That she might bump into him on the street gave her a breathless thrill the ῾῾ *enced* ῾῾ *nce the last time she'd seen* Henri Lejardin.

Yes, there were lots of *who, what, when, where* and *why*s she wanted to ask him. All in good time.

She was glad she'd have the opportunity to work through it before she found herself face-to-face with the man who broke her heart.

Work it out now and get over it.

"You dated him?" A.J. asked.

Margeaux shrugged. "It was a long time ago. We were just kids. We grew up next door to each other."

"And you let him get away?" Pepper stared at her with big, astonished eyes. "Honey, are you out of your mind? If a fine man like that lived next door to me, I don't think I'd bother to leave the grounds. Except for the occasions when I found myself next door borrowing a cup of sugar. And I'm afraid I'd need lots and lots of sugar."

Dear Reader,

I've always been intrigued by reunion stories: tales about couples who once had a connection, but for one reason or another couldn't make their relationship work the first time around. It always seems extrasweet when they meet again years later and finally get it right.

That's the case with Henri and Margeaux, the hero and heroine of *Accidental Heiress*. These childhood sweethearts never got over each other. However, even after their reunion, fate throws a few hurdles in the way. Before they get their second shot at happily ever after, they have to revisit the past and set the record straight. Doing this involves unloading some heavy baggage and entrusting each other with a life-changing secret. But, hey, baggage and secrets are no match for true love. Right?

Please let me know what you think. I love to hear from readers. You can reach me at nrobardsthompson@yahoo.com.

Warmly,

Nancy Robards Thompson

ACCIDENTAL HEIRESS

NANCY ROBARDS THOMPSON

SPECIAL EDITION®

Published by Silhouette Books

America's Publisher of Contemporary Romance

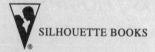 SILHOUETTE BOOKS

ISBN-13: 978-0-373-65564-9

Recycling programs
for this product may
not exist in your area.

ACCIDENTAL HEIRESS

Visit Silhouette Books at www.eHarlequin.com

Printed in U.S.A.

Books by Nancy Robards Thompson

Silhouette Special Edition

Accidental Princess #1931
Accidental Cinderella #2002
*The Family They Chose #2026
Accidental Father #2055
Accidental Heiress #2082

Harlequin NEXT

Out with the Old, In with the New
What Happens in Paris (Stays in Paris?)
Sisters
True Confessions of the Stratford Park PTA
Like Mother, Like Daughter (But in a Good Way)
   "Becoming My Mother..."
Beauty Shop Tales
An Angel in Provence

*The Baby Chase

NANCY ROBARDS THOMPSON

Award-winning author Nancy Robards Thompson is a sister, wife and mother who has lived the majority of her life south of the Mason-Dixon line. As the oldest sibling, she reveled in her ability to make her brother laugh at inappropriate moments, and she soon learned she could get away with it by proclaiming "What? I wasn't doing anything." It's no wonder that upon graduating from college with a degree in journalism, she discovered that reporting "just the facts" bored her silly. Since hanging up her press pass to write novels full-time, critics have deemed her books "funny, smart and observant." She loves chocolate, champagne, cats and art (though not necessarily in that order). When she's not writing, she enjoys spending time with her family, reading, hiking and doing yoga.

This book is dedicated to Claire Borkert,
you are a bright light and inspiration to our family.

Acknowledgments

Caroline Phipps, thank you from the bottom of my heart
for your willingness to read at a moment's notice
and your spot-on editorial advice.

Teresa Brown, thank you for always being there to
help lead me out of the corners I've plotted myself into.

Catherine Kean, thank you for all the years of critiquing.

Boundless gratitude to Gail Chasan and Sarah McDaniel.

I don't know what I'd do without "all y'all!"

Chapter One

"Margeaux, wasn't this guy your boyfriend?"

Boyfriend? Margeaux Broussard chewed a piece of cinnamon gum and leaned against the hotel balcony rail, peering through the viewfinder of her camera, focusing on St. Michel's rocky shoreline. It had been years since she'd had a man in her life—significant or otherwise.

She pressed the shutter release button and the camera snapped a series of rapid shots. The fleeting twilight gilding St. Michel with molten gold was too gorgeous to pass up for the man *du jour* her friend Caroline Coopersmith was talking about…on television…or somewhere in their hotel room. From Margeaux's perch on the hotel balcony, she had a breathtaking panoramic view of the landscape. The light was perfect, and it would be gone in a moment. She wanted to get these shots.

Clickclickclickclick.

"If it is, he looks downright dangerous," Caroline continued.

Clickclickclickclick.

Dangerous?

Margeaux turned and glanced through the open balcony doors at her friend, who was sitting on the bed reading the complimentary issue of *Folio de St. Michel* magazine that had been on the coffee table in their hotel room when they'd checked in earlier that afternoon.

"Let me see," demanded Pepper Meriweather, as she and A. J. Sherwood-Antonelli crowded onto the bed on either side of Caroline and gaped at the picture.

Margeaux turned back to the vista and snapped a few more shots, but the magical light was already fading. At least she'd claimed the best of it.

A.J. let loose an unladylike catcall, which piqued Margeaux's curiosity enough to make her smile, turn back toward her friends and squint at the bold captions on the magazine cover. The words jumped around on the page, and Margeaux had a hard time focusing her dyslexic gaze. She stepped back into the room, refocused on the words, and redoubled her effort to read the print on the magazine cover.

Ahh, it was the magazine's annual "A List" edition, a roll call of her home town's most eligible movers and shakers. Since this was the first time in sixteen years that she'd been back to St. Michel, it would be interesting to see if she knew anyone on the list. She set her camera on the table and prepared to join the ogling party.

"Oooh, dangerous and *delicious,*" Pepper purred, smacking her lips as if she tasted the mystery man in her Southern-laced words. "I'll bet women fall all over themselves for a bite of those honey buns."

"Who is it?" Margeaux asked.

A.J. thrust the periodical toward Margeaux. "Henri Lejardin. Do you know him?"

The name made Margeaux's breath hitch.

"Henri?" Her stomach clenched. Then the bottom of her belly nearly fell out when, there, in living color with his dark, curly hair and penetrating chocolate eyes, her first love smiled at her from the glossy pages of *Folio de St. Michel.*

"Is this him?" Caroline asked.

Margeaux nodded. It was Henri, alright. All grown up and looking fine; different, but somehow still the same.

If he was on the *Folio* list, that meant he was single. It shouldn't matter after all these years, she reminded herself. But it did. Suddenly, she wanted to know everything about him—what he'd been doing all these years; who he was involved with—past and present. Where he was right this very minute. If she knew, she just might go to him and ask him all these questions and others that had plagued her all these years. The fact that she could—that for once, she could walk right out the door and go to him—that she might bump into him on the street—gave her a breathless thrill the likes of which she hadn't experienced since…since the last time she saw Henri Lejardin.

Yes, there were lots of *who, what, when, where and whys* she wanted to ask him. All in good time.

She was bound to run into him, and she needed to prepare herself for the deluge of emotions she was certain to feel, because this simple photo in a magazine already had her hyperventilating. She was glad she'd have the opportunity to work through it before she found herself face-to-face with the man who'd broken her heart.

Work it out now and get over it.

"You dated him?" A.J. asked.

Margeaux shrugged, unable to tear her gaze away from Henri's photo. "It was a long time ago. We were just kids. We grew up next door to each other."

"And you let him get away?" Pepper stared at her with big, astonished eyes. "Honey, are you out of your mind? If a man like that lived next door to me, I don't think I'd bother to leave the grounds. Except for the occasions when I found myself next door borrowing a cup of sugar. And I'm afraid I'd need lots and lots of sugar."

A.J. and Caroline murmured their agreement.

Her history with Henri was complicated. There wasn't an easy way to answer her friends' questions without awakening a lot of sleeping memories, which, her heart warned her, were much better left alone.

Margeaux had been friends with the three women since their junior year in high school at LeClaire Academy, one of the boarding schools to which her father had packed her off after her mother died. The four of them liked to joke that the reason Margeaux had raised such hell getting herself kicked out of the French boarding school she'd attended before LeClaire Academy was because she was simply making her way to Texas so that she could complete their quartet—be the fourth leg of their table.

But now that they were in St. Michel, they were a long way from Texas—and light years away from their rambunctious high school days. The four of them were like family, but the one thing Pepper, A.J. and Caroline didn't know about their friend was that she'd harbored a secret for as long as she'd known them. And that secret, which she'd relegated to the deep recesses of her mind and heart, was doing its very best to push its way out into the golden St. Michel sun.

"I'm guessing if he's in that magazine, it means he's still local," Pepper said. "Why don't you call him and invite him to meet us down in the casino tonight?"

Margeaux took one last wistful look at Henri's broad smile before closing the magazine and turning the figurative lock on the emotions that threatened to overwhelm her. She didn't need the sharp reminder of what happened when she allowed her heart to lead her past the point of no return. She was a grown woman now, and she had no intention of backtracking down that fateful path.

"I can't go to the casino tonight," she said. "But you all go ahead without me. I have to go to the hospital to visit my father, and I don't know how long I'll be. If he's well enough to talk, I have a feeling we'll spend a lot of time catching up. If he's not…I'll need to sit with him."

Her father was the reason she found herself

back in St. Michel after all this time. They'd been estranged for more years than she could count on both hands. But all it took was a call to tell her that her father was in the hospital— that he'd suffered a stroke—and she'd been on a plane to him. No more oceans between them. All the harsh words fired like weapons were forgotten. It was a new chapter. Margeaux was grateful it wasn't too late. Sure, he'd been absent from her life all those years. But one of them had to be the first to extend the olive branch.

She might as well be the one.

"You can join us after you do that," Pepper insisted.

"Pepper, don't," A.J. reprimanded. "This isn't a pleasure trip for Margeaux and the last thing she needs right now is you nagging her to shirk responsibility."

Despite how much she wanted to wave off what A.J. was saying, her friend was right. Margeaux hadn't come here on vacation. Her father needed her to step up and do the right thing. It had been so long since she'd been the good daughter—actually, had she ever attempted that role? If she had, maybe he wouldn't have sent her away all those years ago.

Now that he was sick, all the rules were changing. She was the prodigal daughter returned home. Even though her friends had accompanied her this far, she had to make the next leg of the journey—the trip to the hospital—alone.

Henri Lejardin glanced at the screen of his BlackBerry: one missed call.

Earlier, when his phone rang, he'd been in the middle of a Musée du St. Michel staff meeting, firming up specifics for the Impressionist Retrospective's exhibition, which would celebrate the museum's centennial anniversary. It had been a long day overseeing the installation of the exhibit on loan from museums from all across Europe. The collection was set to open next week. Yet three key paintings were detained in customs, held back by a mountain of red tape Henri had yet to unravel. His career and reputation hinged on this show, and since it was coming down to the wire, he needed to focus on pulling it together.

When his brother Luc's number had appeared

on the screen, Henri had sensed what the call was about, resisted the urge to answer and let it go to voice mail.

Now that the meeting had adjourned, he remained at the conference room table and listened to his messages.

"Henri, it's Luc. Please call me as soon as possible. Margeaux Broussard is back in St. Michel."

Henri's insides shifted like falling dominos and he tightened his grip on the phone, a visceral reaction to the news.

It was exactly the message he'd both feared and anticipated since the moment Colbert Broussard had fallen ill.

As he disconnected from voice mail and dialed Luc, Sydney James, the gallery curator, caught his eye as she lingered in the conference room doorway. A slow, seductive smile spread over her red-glossed lips as she arched a well-shaped brow.

It was a look that suggested so much more than Henri could deal with right now. In an attempt to own his composure, he shook his head and looked away. As the phone rang, he pushed away from the table in the rolling leather chair, leaned back and stretched his legs out in front of him. A posture that suggested he was perfectly at ease. Even though he wasn't.

Fake it until you make it had always been his motto, and it had served him well, considering he was St. Michel's youngest Minister of Arts, Culture and Education. His next goal was to become the youngest member of the Crown Council—St. Michel's version of Parliament. All in due time. First, he had to get his brother on the phone and find out the particulars of Margeaux Broussard's visit.

"Henri?" Luc's anxious voice sounded through the BlackBerry. "I've been trying to reach you."

"I know. I'm sorry; I've been in meetings all day. I got your message. So, she's here?"

To steady himself, Henri doodled on the legal pad in the cordovan leather folio that lay open on the table.

"Yes, she is. She and three friends arrived today around eleven and they checked into a suite at the Hotel de St. Michel."

As Henri wrote the words *Margeaux— Hotel de St. Michel,* he sensed someone reading over his shoulder. He looked up and there was Sydney staring down at his notes.

"Hold on a moment, Luc." Henri closed the folio and took the phone away from his ear. "I'll catch up with you as soon as I'm finished."

She regarded him for a moment. Her predatory gaze meandered the length of his body. She bit her bottom lip.

"I'll wait for you in the Ferdinand Gallery."

Her proper British accent was a strange juxtaposition to the seductive glint in her wide-set green eyes, which stirred an uncomfortable, *not-at-work* reaction in Henri that made him want to retreat.

But he didn't. He simply frowned and shook his head—trying to remind her that he was the boss. Games like this were not okay. They'd had that discussion more than once in the month since he'd allowed the lines of propriety to blur.

True to form, Sydney winked and turned away, her snug black pencil skirt—wasn't that what they called those body-hugging contraptions that accentuated all the right curves in all the right places?—an animated reminder of why he'd made an exception to his no-fraternizing rule for Sydney James.

She was a beautiful woman and a force to be reckoned with. There was no doubt about that. Normally, he went to great lengths to keep his personal and professional lives separate—especially when it came to getting involved with subordinates. But Sydney had a way of pushing the envelope and crossing lines—if she wasn't so damn good at her job Henri might consider having her relocated to a department not under his watch.

That would make matters so much simpler.

But the truth was he needed her. In more than one way. Certain members of the Crown Council had been breathing down his neck, suggesting it was time for him to settle down, to tidy up his personal life so that the other, more traditional, council members—namely Colbert Broussard—would take him seriously as a future Crown Council candidate.

Sydney was professional enough to bolster his reputation, sexy enough to hold his attention and smart enough to know when to turn up the heat or tone it down.

Henri resumed his phone call.

As Sydney turned the corner at the end of the long corridor that led away from the boardroom, she glanced back over her shoulder and gave Henri *that look*. He might not be in love with her. But he sure did appreciate her...*assets*. What was even better was his lust was tempered by a healthy dose of respect for her. The woman had style, an Oxford education, and a way of gracefully walking that fine line between *vaah-vaah-vaah-voom* and put-you-in-your-place business smarts.

What more could he want?

"Margeaux Broussard."

Yes, Margeaux. Wait— "What?"

"We were talking about Margeaux," said Luc.

Henri cleared his throat and raked a hand through his hair.

"Yes, we were."

It had been a long time since that heady August sixteen years ago when Margeaux had left. She'd taken his heart and never looked back. They'd been teenagers. Their heads had been full of idealistic notions and their hearts had been ruled by hormones.

It had been a long time ago, and just because

she was back—well, now they were twice the age they'd been when they'd last seen each other. Surely, they were different people who'd grown in different directions.

"Will you see her?" Luc asked.

Henri drew a three-dimensional box around the words he'd written on the yellow legal pad. Then he retraced the letters M-A-R-G-E-A-U-X.

She was back in St. Michel. And sooner than he'd expected, considering he'd had his doubts about whether she'd show up at all. Honestly, the last thing he needed was Margeaux Broussard dropping their weighty baggage in the middle of his already chaotic life.

"Henri, are you there?" His brother Luc asked.

"Yes, I'm here. Of course I'll try to contact her. But that doesn't mean she wants to see me."

Henri didn't mean to sound so testy. After all, his brother had done him a favor by directing the chief of the Bureau of Customs to alert him when Margeaux arrived.

"But I'm going to try," Henri added, purposely shaving the edge off his tone.

Luc had been in charge of St. Michel's national security before he married Sophie Baldwin, the woman who was the newly crowned queen of St. Michel. Despite stepping into a head-of-state position, Luc still had his fingers on the pulse of the country's security, and had happily helped out his brother when he'd been asked.

"I'm sure Colbert will be happy Margeaux's home," Luc said. "It sounds like he's going to need some help once he gets out of the hospital."

Henri blew out a breath.

A lot had changed, but a lot remained the same—such as the way his heart beat a faster cadence at the mention of her name.

Even so he reminded himself that Margeaux hadn't come home for him.

That was a thought that was oddly more disappointing than helpful.

After finishing the call with Luc, Henri made his way to the Ferdinand Gallery where Sydney had said she'd be waiting for him. He glanced around, but she wasn't there.

He contemplated telling her to behave

herself—to quit flirting. However, knowing
Sydney, that would only encourage her. Instead,
he decided to leave well enough alone and
focus on more pressing matters such as how
to expedite the rest of the paintings through
French customs. They'd been on loan to a museum in Brussels and the orders to have them
shipped straight to St. Michel should've been
clear, but the paintings had mistakenly been
returned to Paris. Henri was beginning to think
that it might have been faster to pick them up
at the Musée d'Orsay and bring them to St.
Michel himself rather than wait for a bunch
of bureaucrats to unravel the unnecessary red
tape binding the priceless works of art.

He walked over and straightened one of
the Monets already in place—a landscape of
a house and overgrown garden that reminded
him of the Broussards' home with the sprawl-
ing terrace and thick, wild orchard where he'd
spent so much of his youth. His thoughts flew
to Margeaux, and her father's situation.

Colbert could've hired home healthcare, and
he had friends and staff who would've ensured
that he was cared for. The man wouldn't have
been left high and dry. Still, Henri was one-

quarter surprised Margeaux had come home and three-quarters relieved. It was nice to know that she'd come when her father needed her.

Because he wasn't so sure the woman he'd read about in the tabloids over the past sixteen years would have made the trip. That tabloid heiress, who'd been estranged from her family and friends for more than a decade and a half, hardly resembled the girl who'd once been his best friend and first lover.

"You're a million miles away from that Monet, love," whispered a soft feminine voice. It made him jump. When he turned to face Sydney, she flashed that broad, sexy smile that usually coaxed a return grin from him. Today, however, her charms weren't working.

"I was just taking a mental inventory of all that we have left to do before the exhibit opens."

Her gaze locked with his and her mouth turned down into a slight frown. Arching a brow that seemed to convey that she didn't believe him, she said. "Oh, you mean all those things we discussed in the meeting? I took excellent notes. I'll send you a copy, so you don't have to worry."

He'd always found her attractive, and most of the time he found her no-holds-barred approach appealing. But for some reason, today, it was off-putting, too much for the workplace. The closer she got, the more claustrophobic he felt. It was as if she were backing him into a corner. He fought the urge to step back, to put some space between them. Instead, he turned back to the painting and studied it.

"What do you think?" he asked. "Do we want to keep it here or should we move it across the way?"

He pointed toward the shorter wall on the other side of the room.

"So, you're not going to tell me," she said.

"Tell you what?" Henri asked.

"Who this person is who has shanghaied your thoughts?"

Henri crossed his arms.

"It's a family matter. I don't want to discuss it at work."

Sydney's green eyes darkened a shade, and she shrugged.

"I'm sorry," she said. "I didn't mean to pry. I was simply concerned about you."

She reached up to touch his hand, but he

uncrossed his arms and shoved his fists into his trouser pockets, dodging the contact.

Sydney flinched. "Henri?"

He lowered his voice. "That's not what we should do here."

She blinked once. Twice.

"What I mean is we agreed to keep matters strictly platonic at work."

"Yes, of course we did." Suddenly all business, she was the one who took a step backward. Henri sensed the transformation immediately. "I'll be in my office reviewing the PDF of the show catalogue." With that, she turned and walked away. He was amazed at how fast her demeanor could change. One minute the flirt, the next the serious businesswoman.

Henri felt that old familiar inner riptide of uncertainty, which should've been reason enough to let her keep walking. Even if Sydney had been pushing the bounds of what was appropriate in the workplace, at least she knew when to rein it in.

Unlike Margeaux, who had created a reputation for herself as a socialite run amok. She seemed to take pleasure in embarrassing her father with her headline-grabbing antics. Even if she had been lying low for the past couple of years, her reputation preceded her. *Fille sauvage,* her father had called her for as far back as Henri could remember. As if living up to the label her father had slapped on her, Margeaux Broussard had, indeed, proven herself every bit the *wild child.*

Not the type of woman he needed to get involved with if the Crown Council was ever going to take him seriously.

"Sydney, wait."

She stopped underneath the archway that led into the main gallery, but she didn't turn around.

Henri knew he'd hurt her feelings. He hadn't meant to. He was simply skittish about public displays of affection at work, even if it was simply the brush of a hand or an I-want-you pucker of lips. He expected no less of his other employees. He had to lead by example.

"Please let me know when you hear about the missing pieces for the catalogue," she said, without looking back at him. "If we don't get this to the printer by Wednesday, we won't have the catalogue in time for the opening."

He glanced around. They were the only ones in the gallery.

"If you're free tonight, perhaps we could have some dinner and proof them…together. Two sets of eyes are always better than one."

This time she turned around and faced him, that devilishly sexy left brow of hers rising, a question mark. She crossed her arms over her chest, creating a barrier between them.

"A business meeting?" she asked. "After hours?"

She wasn't going to make this easy.

Still, he nodded.

"I suppose that might work," she said. "But I have one stipulation. I want to go out—to Le Coeur Bleu in the Hotel de St. Michel."

The Hotel de St. Michel. Where Margeaux was staying. No doubt she'd read his notes about the Hotel St. Michel. It was too much of a coincidence otherwise.

It was a bad idea to bring Sydney there, even though the chance they'd run into Margeaux and her friends was remote. He should go there alone. He should contact Margeaux and arrange a private meeting….

Even so, as he opened his mouth to suggest a different restaurant, he heard himself agreeing, "Le Coeur Bleu it is."

Chapter Two

Margeaux paused in the hospital hallway, a death grip on the bouquet of colorful flowers. The door to room 436 was ajar, and classical music drifted through the scant opening. She drew in a steadying breath of antiseptic-smelling hospital air and summoned her strength. On the other side of the door was the man she hadn't seen in more than sixteen years.

Her father.

She was an accomplished photographer. She'd put herself through college and had taken herself all over the world.

But standing there, about to see her father for the first time after all the years and bad blood that had passed between them, she was suddenly desperate for her father's approval.

Sadly, she wasn't entirely sure he'd be glad to see her.

She was so nervous she couldn't get a good breath, and for a heartbeat, she was paralyzed—right there in the hallway as the nurses and orderlies passed by with purpose. One of Margeaux's hands held the flowers like a torch; the other was frozen in mid-knock as a deluge of emotions and questions rained down on her.

Run!

Turn and run!

But this is your father. He's sick. He needs you.

Right, he's never needed you. What if he doesn't want to see you? What if he sends you away again?

Suddenly, she felt sixteen again, awkward and unsure of where she fit into the life of her only living relative. A girl out of control, starving for the acceptance of a self-involved father who was too busy to deal with her antics.

But she wasn't a child anymore, and it had been at least three years since the press had skewered her with scandal.

Knock.

Her hand did just that. As if on its own, her knuckles sounded a quick *tap-tap-tap* on the door.

"Qui?" What? barked a gruff voice from inside. Her breath caught, icy in her chest, and a rush of adrenaline urged her away. *Run! Go! Leave now!*

"Papa, it's me." The voice sounded as if it came from outside herself, but it was her own. Then for the span of several heartbeats all she could hear was the blood rushing in her ears. Until the gruff voice softened and asked almost tentatively, "Margeaux? Is it you?"

Her fingertips grazed the door's cool wood surface as she pushed the door open a hair and looked in.

"Why are you lurking out there in the hallway?" The voice was gruff again. "Come in here."

Before her feet could carry her in the opposite direction, she pushed the door open the rest of the way, and found herself face-to-face with her father. Unsure of what to do—whether to sit or stand, whether to hug him or hang back—she simply stood there and drank him in.

His once dark, full head of hair was thinner and silvery white. His cheeks were hollow and his previously strong, proud shoulders appeared rounded. Hooked up to IV bags, pulse monitors and a host of other machines, he looked wizened and frail, but the fire in his dark brown eyes burned strong, belying time's havoc.

She tried to see past the lines time had etched on her father's face. She tried to ignore the creases around his eyes and the wisps of silver hair. She tried to see past the lost years and the pain of rejection to the possibility of new beginnings. He needed her. She was here. Wasn't that enough?

Please let that be enough.

"Come in and shut the door," he insisted. "No use allowing the entire ward to gawk at us."

As if paying penance for the obedient child she'd never been, Margeaux found herself submissively closing the door and turning back to him, still unsure of what to do with herself.

"Come over here so I can see you." The commanding tone of his voice was just as strong as the fire of self possession that blazed in his gaze. As she approached his bed, her father's gaze took her in, but his expression did not betray an ounce of approval. In fact, he watched her so stoically she wondered if he even saw her, or if, as had usually been the case, he was looking right through her, toward his own affairs. Immersed in a world that had always taken him away from her.

Finally, his eyes locked onto hers—a steel trap closing around her heart, and they stared at each other for a long moment. Margeaux didn't know what to do with her hands, so she wrapped her arms around her middle as if to keep herself from falling apart. She stood there searching his face for something, anything. A sign to tell her how to proceed.

Breaking the ice was the hardest part, she reassured herself. She'd been giving herself a pep talk from the moment she'd decided to come home: *Everything will be fine as soon as we make it past...this.*

Margeaux tried to ignore the voice inside

that asked, *would it be fine? Why would it be fine now when it had never been fine before?*

"Sit down." Colbert pointed to a chair adjacent to the bed. That's when she noticed his hand was shaking. Maybe this wasn't easy for him, either. Or maybe it was the effects of the stroke.

Either way, it was unsettling.

Margeaux settled herself in the chair and smoothed her cotton turquoise skirt.

"Tell me, what are you doing these days?" her father demanded.

"I'm a photographer."

He pursed his lips as if a bad taste had assaulted his mouth.

"So you've turned the tables, *eh?* Now, *you're* the one taking the photographs rather than serving as the paparazzi's favorite subject."

Then something miraculous happened: he smiled.

And Margeaux could breathe again.

"Oh, Papa, how are you?" She ignored the sting of tears. She wouldn't cry. She couldn't allow herself that luxury because her father would see that as a weakness. And things were going so well.

He shrugged. "Other than being irritated and inconvenienced by being here, I'm fine. In fact, they say I'll probably be released tomorrow."

"That's great news!" He must not be as sick as he looked.

He waved away her joy. "Lord knows, I don't have time to spend one more day in this place. I told them if they kept me here I'd probably end up killing myself. So, they're smart and are doing the right thing by releasing me."

Margeaux frowned. He'd had a stroke and was darn lucky the episode hadn't set him back any more than this. His body might be showing the wear of time and toil, but his will was stronger than ever. Impatient as ever. Obviously, that hadn't changed. Maybe that's why he was in here. In fact, given the lethal combination of high-stress politics, mixed with his explosive temper, she was surprised he hadn't found himself in the hospital before. This was a warning he needed to heed. He'd only been in the hospital less than a week, and it seemed awfully fast for him to be going home after suffering a stroke.

"Dad, don't be stubborn. When it comes to your health, you shouldn't push it. Business will wait. The Crown Council won't make any important decisions without you. The only thing that matters is that you rest and allow your body time to heal."

Again, he waved her off. But this time he seemed too tired to argue the point. He simply turned his head and gazed out the window.

Pink and violet hues of twilight painted the sky, which was crowded with cumulus clouds gilded molten by the setting sun. The window framed the melancholy scene, provoking an air of sadness in Margeaux.

There was something about twilight—that limbo between day and night—that had always unsettled Margeaux. She wasn't sure if the pull of sadness tugging at her was because of that or her father's aloofness.

He'd always been aloof. Now, the two were virtual strangers since they'd been estranged for so many years. Margeaux knew her antics certainly hadn't helped them bond, though until he'd made the quip about her being the tabloids' favorite subject she hadn't been certain he'd ever seen any of the sensationalized stories, since his responses to the press were usually,

"I don't know what you're talking about," or a steely "No comment."

Now they were face-to-face, trying to reach each other over a rickety bridge of years suspended precariously over oceans of differences. But when she'd decided to come back to St. Michel she'd resigned herself to the fact that it wouldn't be easy.

He was sick and this wasn't about her or the past. All that mattered was what happened from this moment forward.

"I'm sure you'll understand that I need to talk to your doctor as soon as possible. If for no other reason than to make sure I understand your care plan?"

He didn't answer her, and a food-service attendant broke the silence when she entered with a tray.

"Good evening, Monsieur Broussard," she said. "I certainly hope you're hungry. Tonight's meal is a treat—chicken scaloppini. You're going to love it."

She offered him a broad grin as she set the tray on the bed table and rolled it in front of him. "And who is this lovely lady?"

Her father stiffened ever so slightly. It was

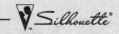

SPECIAL EDITION

USA TODAY BESTSELLING AUTHOR

MARIE FERRARELLA

**BRINGS YOU ANOTHER
HEARTWARMING STORY FROM**

When Lilli McCall disappeared on him
after he proposed, Kullen Manetti swore
never to fall in love again. Eight years later
Lilli is back in his life, threatening to break
down all the walls he's put up to
safeguard his heart.

UNWRAPPING
THE PLAYBOY

*Available December
wherever books are sold.*

Silhouette *Desire*

USA TODAY bestselling authors

MAUREEN CHILD

and

SANDRA HYATT

UNDER THE MILLIONAIRE'S MISTLETOE

Just when these leading men thought they had it all figured out, they quickly learn their hearts have made other plans. Two passionate stories about love, longing and the infinite possibilities of kissing under the mistletoe.

Available December wherever you buy books.

Always Powerful, Passionate and Provocative.

coming to my rescue."

He tensed. Neighbor? *What neighbor kisses you like I did?* "That's me, just the full-service landlord," he said, trying to keep the sarcasm out of his voice. He started to leave, but she put her hand on his arm.

"Jarrett, what I meant was you went beyond helping me." Her eyes searched his face. "I've asked far too much of you."

"Did you hear me complain?"

She shook her head. "You should. I feel like I've taken advantage."

"Like I said, I haven't minded."

"And I'm grateful for everything…"

Grasping her hand on his arm, Jarrett leaned forward. The memory of last night's kiss had him aching for another. "I didn't do it for your gratitude, Mia."

Gorgeous tycoon Jarrett McKane has never believed in Christmas—but he can't help being drawn to soon-to-be-mom Mia Saunders! Christmases past were spent alone…and now Jarrett may just have a fairy-tale ending for all his Christmases future!

Available December 2010,
only from Harlequin® Romance®.

See below for a sneak peek from our classic
Harlequin® Romance® line.

Introducing DADDY BY CHRISTMAS by Patricia Thayer.

MIA caught sight of Jarrett when he walked into the open lobby. It was hard not to notice the man. In a charcoal business suit with a crisp white shirt and striped tie covered by a dark trench coat, he looked more Wall Street than small-town Colorado.

Mia couldn't blame him for keeping his distance. He was probably tired of taking care of her.

Besides, why would a man like Jarrett McKane be interested in her? Why would he want to take on a woman expecting a baby? Yet he'd done so many things for her. He'd been there when she'd needed him most. How could she not care about a man like that?

Heart pounding in her ears, she walked up behind him. Jarrett turned to face her. "Did you get enough sleep last night?"

"Yes, thanks to you," she said, wondering if he'd thought about their kiss. Her gaze went to his mouth, then she quickly glanced away. "And thank you for not bringing up my meltdown."

Jarrett couldn't stop looking at Mia. Blue was definitely her color, bringing out the richness of her eyes.

"What meltdown?" he said, trying hard to focus on what she was saying. "You were just exhausted from lack of sleep and worried about your baby."

He couldn't help remembering how, during the night, he'd kept going in to watch her sleep. How strange was that? "I hope you got enough rest."

She nodded. "Plenty. And you're a good neighbor for

so subtle that it would've gone unnoticed by most, but Margeaux saw the reflex. She wasn't sure if he was reacting to the woman's acting so familiar or if he was embarrassed by Margeaux.

"Hi, I'm his daughter, Margeaux Broussard."

"My name is Nadine. So nice to meet you. For some reason, I was under the impression that the Monsieur did not have family…or at least none close by."

"Well, I'm all he has. I live in Texas right now, but I came as fast as I could when I learned my father had taken ill."

"So good of you to come and care for him."

Colbert cleared his throat, "Excuse me, my dinner is not getting any warmer. Would you please allow me to enjoy it before it becomes any more unpalatable?"

Nadine gave a quick nod and excused herself, and Margeaux settled back into her seat, waiting for him to uncover the tray and take the first bite.

Instead, he cleared his throat again.

"You should go, too."

His dismissal was formal and impatient.

"Why? I want to stay with you while you eat."

He shook his head. "You watching me eat would be awkward. Please go. You may come back tomorrow and take me home."

Margeaux stood, not wanting to leave. He was sending her away so that he could eat dinner alone. She wondered if she should push or comply. He'd always been blunt. In fact, the thing about Colbert Broussard was he always said what he meant—for better or worse. Her mother, Alice, had always been the buffer between father and daughter, smoothing the rough edges of his candid comments. After she died, things fell apart.

In hindsight, Margeaux knew both she and her father had been devastated by her death. But at the time, she'd felt lost and alone. A motherless sixteen-year-old and a despondent widower—not a good recipe for a functional family.

She wondered if Henri, who had once been like the son her father never had, had looked in on him. But the last she knew, her father had banished Henri, too.

Now was not the time to open that box.

Later.

They'd have plenty of time to sort that out in the coming months.

Colbert picked up his knife and fork and carved a small bit of chicken, but he set down his fork rather than taking a bite.

"There's nothing you can do tonight. The doctor won't make his rounds until tomorrow, and it will be too uncomfortable for me if you sit there and watch me eat. So go. Come back tomorrow, when you'll have a purpose for being here. Tomorrow, you'll take me home."

Having been relieved of her hospital duty, Margeaux got back to the hotel earlier than she'd expected. She'd left her father only because he'd insisted. She left because she didn't want to fight with him.

Surrender. That was the name of the game right now. All in the name of keeping the peace. She hadn't come here to fight. She'd come to make things right.

Tomorrow morning, she and the girls would wind their way up the serpentine road to Margeaux's childhood home and get the place

ready for her father's homecoming later that afternoon.

Tonight, she was free to enjoy herself.

Though it felt a little wrong to be planning a night in the casino while her father was laid up in the hospital, that's exactly what she intended to do. The alternative was to spend the evening holed up in her room. That wouldn't do anyone any good.

Her friends had come with her to act as backup support. Though they understood the situation—on all levels—she wanted to show them how much she appreciated them circling the wagons. They'd met by chance but had remained friends by choice. They were the sisters she'd chosen. Tonight was the perfect opportunity to show them a good time St. Michel–style.

Margeaux had called them on her way back to the hotel. They graciously waited as she raced to clean up and put on one of the many dresses that Pepper had carted over.

"So, now you're happy I *overpacked*." Pepper clapped like a child who'd just found the prize at the bottom of the Cracker Jack box. She addressed her comments to no one in particular,

everyone in general. "If I'd been the *practical* traveler that y'all had tried to convert me into, just imagine the fix we'd be in right now."

"Oh, horrors, we might've had to go *shopping* so that Margeaux could look presentable." Caroline sipped champagne from a crystal flute. "Imagine that."

The number of bags Pepper Meriweather had brought might suggest that she intended to stay for the summer, rather than the planned two weeks.

Right now, the fifteen evening dresses and twenty-five pairs of shoes and sandals Pepper couldn't leave home without were proving to be a lifesaver.

Margeaux chose a slinky little black dress and a pair of sexy, strappy sandals to complement it. As they made their way down to the casino, she caught a glimpse of her reflection in the mirrored hallway leading to the grand lobby of the Hotel de St. Michel. It had been a while since she'd dressed for a night out. Pepper had styled Margeaux's long, blond hair into a chignon that looked as if she'd gone to the salon.

The sexy black dress made Margeaux's skin

look a little paler than she would've liked, but she'd been working so much lately that she hadn't had time to build the deep bronze glow that had been her trademark.

Even so, seeing her reflection made her check her posture and hold her head a little higher. She was still pushing against the inner struggle of whether going down to the casino was the right thing to do with her father in the hospital. It smacked of fodder for tabloid headlines: Margeaux Broussard Parties while Father Lies in Hospital Bed. Tonight, the only thing better than being anonymous would be rendering herself invisible. But her father was fine. She'd done her duty by him tonight and would follow his wishes to come back and get him tomorrow.

Besides, this dress was far too fabulous for invisible.

Bottom line: Margeaux Broussard had never shied away from life, and she didn't intend to start now. Tonight would simply be a nice night out with friends.

Nothing scandalous about that.

"We all look like Bond girls," said A.J. "I

wonder if we'll meet any spies in the casino tonight?"

The girls laughed and as they forged ahead toward the casino, Margeaux hung back in the lobby, reacquainting herself with the hotel's ornate beauty. The chandeliers hung from frescoed ceilings, dripping honeyed light, warming the gold-and-marble atrium. She took in the sculptures, the caryatids and the bas-relief motifs etched into the walls.

Throughout her youth, she'd seen this place dozens of times. The memory had her gaze shifting until she'd located a certain long, dark hallway that led to one of the seven elevator banks.

Once on a dare, she'd dragged Henri here; they were only thirteen years old and he was her best friend. They'd hid in the hallway with a bag containing a big, black rattle snake, which he'd trapped in the overgrown orchard that grew between her homes. She'd dared him to let it loose in the lobby during the high-season rush.

He didn't want to, but she'd taunted him until he'd buckled.

"Okay, I will on one condition," he'd said,

and Margeaux had been too full of mischief to even ask about the *condition*. How bad could it be if he was too chicken to do something like this? All she wanted was for Henri Lejardin, son of the Minister of Security and Protocol, to break out of his shell and do something *fun* for a change.

She didn't care if they got caught. The worst that would happen was that it would rile up her father. Sure, it would embarrass him if it came to light that his daughter had a hand in the prank.

But shouldn't a man who had no time for his family feel a little embarrassment? At least he'd have to make time for her—even if it was to reprimand her.

But Margeaux's father wasn't the only one who'd gotten a surprise that day. After Henri had set the snake free in the lobby and Margeaux had sufficiently delighted in the way people had screamed and scattered like handfuls of tossed marbles, Henri had run back to the dark hallway, backed her against the wall and kissed her senseless. She'd never seen it coming. She'd certainly never thought a boy

who played by all the rules would ever do something so bold and out of character.

The unexpected feel of his mouth on hers had sent her reeling. She could remember it as vividly as if it had happened yesterday. Henri had kissed her boldly, ravenously, and she'd kissed him back, in awe at his hunger. It was as if they'd both done it before, though neither of them had.

Somehow, following instinct, they just knew what to do.

Over the next three years, instinct would lead them to new, uncharted territory. They'd explored together and discovered just how well they'd fit.

Their hands.

Their mouths.

Their bodies.

Henri was no longer the shy, hesitant one.

Margeaux had liked these new paths down which he coaxed her and she'd followed willingly.

Until finally, they'd reached a dead end.

Now Margeaux felt anxious. Her nerve endings were like live wires, burning under her skin. She put her fingers to her lips,

remembering the feel of that first kiss. More than once when she'd kissed another man, she'd found herself fantasizing that the man was Henri, only to suffer the letdown when she'd opened her eyes to discover the familiar stranger in her arms.

The memory of that first kiss took her back. Tonight it was as if she were seeing everything for the first time, and it had an unforgettable emotional impact.

Henri was somewhere on this island, and she had a sudden urge to find him and rediscover some of those paths.

But the newly discovered rational side of her reminded her that it had been a long time since they'd talked, much less kissed or… He certainly had a life by now. Probably a wife. Maybe even a family.

She hadn't kept up with him because it hurt too much. Too much history, too much…too much. She'd been lying low for the past couple of years trying to play the "out of sight, out of mind" game with the press. It had worked. The paparazzi had finally moved on to the newest *celebutante* train wreck.

Rehabilitating one's self was not "sexy

news." Nobody cared that Margeaux Broussard had finally grown up and was making her own way. That she wasn't stupid—it was dyslexia that had held her back. After that heaven-sent discovery she'd made with Pepper's help, everything had changed. It was as if the world that had always been blurry and nonsensical had finally snapped into focus.

She wasn't stupid. She was sober and productive and some had even deemed her talented. Through photography, she'd finally found her voice and her vision.

That was what had given her the strength to come home. Finally, she could prove to her disapproving father that she wasn't the *fille sauvage*—the wild girl—as he'd written her off. It would take a while, but she was prepared to go the distance.

"Margeaux, come on!" called Caroline. "Hurry up."

The girls waited for her at the entrance to the casino.

She took one last wistful look at the hallway and glanced around the lobby. She'd come back here and photograph the hotel lobby, she decided as she walked toward her friends. This

would be the first of many places and people she intended to get reacquainted with.

Knowing that Margeaux Broussard was back in town made everything about St. Michel feel different to Henri Lejardin.

As he and Sydney entered the lobby of the Hotel du St. Michel, he was glad to have hands full of the materials they'd need to do a final edit of the copy for the show catalogue during their working *date*.

He'd made a final call to the curator of the Musée d'Orsay, pressuring him about the missing paintings. When the curator couldn't assure their arrival by Wednesday, Henri decided to cut the pieces from the show.

It may have been a rash decision, but he'd been impatient all day and wanted closure on this project, so that they could move forward with plans for the opening.

Knowing that Margeaux was back had only added to his anxiousness. He'd kept thinking he was catching glimpses of her out of the corner of his eye. A mane of long, straight, blond hair here, a flash of long, strong, tanned leg there. But they all proved to be specters.

Maybe his rush to tie up loose ends with this show was so he could finally call her and get the inevitable out of the way. When it came to Margeaux, he'd always been reckless and impulsive. Obviously, nothing had changed.

He hadn't seen her in years, but her presence permeated his being like a spirit.

He glanced at Sydney, feeling a little guilty for bringing her here tonight, even if it had been her suggestion and she hadn't budged when he'd recommended other options. If he was fully honest with himself, he hadn't vetoed her choice of meeting location because he *hoped* he'd run into Margeaux.

Tonight.

The sooner the better.

So, it almost came as no surprise when he heard a lovely brunette call from the entrance to the casino, "Margeaux, come on! Hurry up."

He turned his head, and there she was. Looking like a grownup version of the girl he'd once loved so deeply. A vision in a black evening dress, her blond hair smoothed back into a sophisticated up-do that accentuated her crystal blue eyes.

She took a few steps toward her friend, and then her gaze snapped to the right as if he'd called her name.

He hadn't. Not out loud.

It had always been like that between them.

Just as he'd somehow known if he came here tonight, he'd see her.

After a split second of pure joy, his heart sank. What the hell was she doing at the casino her first night in town when her father was in the hospital?

Worse yet, why had he known in his heart he'd find her here?

"Henri? Is that you?" For a moment, Margeaux was frozen in her tracks, but then she found her footing and her legs carried her to him.

He didn't even have to say anything. He simply flashed that smile.

Yes! It is.

And before either could say a word, they were in each other's arms.

The contact was brief but intense and it stole her breath. Even though a lifetime had passed since they'd last seen each other—sixteen years

since they'd last seen each other, at age sixteen—it felt as if there'd never been any space
between them.

They pulled apart and stared at each other.

He was so gorgeous it made her heart hurt.
So did the dawning realization that the beautiful woman standing next to him was the
woman pictured with him in the *Folio de St.
Michel* photo.

"I can't believe it's you," Margeaux said.
"What are you doing here?"

She smiled at him and then at the woman,
her heart aching at the prospect of not knowing who she was or what they meant to each
other. A quick glance at the woman's hand re-
vealed she didn't wear rings—engagement or
wedding.

"Margeaux, I'd heard you were back," he
said. "Oh, excuse me. This is my associate,
Sydney James. She is the curator for one of the
state art museums under my jurisdiction."

The woman flinched at the introduction before artfully covering the slight with a bright
smile and the offer of a handshake.

Not only was she beautiful, but she had an

impeccable British accent that gave her the air of someone proper and well educated.

So, Henri had gotten himself a beauty with brains. That rankled Margeaux even more than the way that Henri had tried to downplay his relationship with his coworker.

They weren't just colleagues. Obviously not from Sydney's—was that her name—point of view.

A.J., Caroline and Pepper joined them, and as Margeaux made the introductions she felt Henri's gaze alternately acknowledge each woman she introduced and then drift back to her.

When the introductions were done, an awkward silence fell over the group, so Margeaux interjected, "I saw my father today and he swiftly kicked me out."

Henri's brows knit. "I'm sorry to hear that."

"Oh, no! It wasn't like that." Margeaux touched his shoulder and she felt Sydney's displeasure rolling off her in palpable waves. "He was actually quite happy to see me. Er, as happy as my father can let on. You know how he is."

Henri of all people would understand. He'd once been so close to her father, but Colbert all but disowned him after *that night.*

The night that had landed her a one-way ticket to the first of a series of boarding schools. But she didn't want to think about that now. It was ancient history and this felt like the dawning of what might be a new era.

Margeaux's thoughts were called back to the present as Henri was explaining to Sydney exactly who her father was.

Margeaux caught an equal mix of reverence and "Oh, you're *that* Margeaux Broussard." The perceived judgment in the woman's expression made Margeaux want to lash out with a *You don't know me. You have no right to judge me.*

But Henri diverted the tension. "Sydney and I are having dinner in the restaurant. Won't you join us?"

Sydney frowned. "What about the catalogue?"

He dismissed her. "We still have several days before it needs to go to the printer. Please join us."

The last thing Margeaux wanted to do was

intrude on their date. No, that wasn't entirely true. She simply didn't want to have dinner with Sydney shooting daggers. She and Henri had a lot to catch up on. And when they did, it should be just the two of them.

"Thank you, but we were heading to the casino. I don't want to come between you and your…project."

Margeaux flashed her friendliest smile at Sydney, who managed to manufacture an equally pleasant expression.

"We will join you for a drink at the casino bar, then," Henri said, and a sense of relief flooded over Margeaux. She wasn't ready to say goodbye to him tonight.

In the same way that she hadn't been ready to say goodbye all those years ago. Even if it was just a drink, it was more time. The rest would work itself out.

"I bought my parents' house," Henri said. "So I still live next door to your father."

The revelation surprised her. "How has that been?" she asked cautiously, not sure if she wanted to hear the answer. At least not right now.

"Your father and I have had our differences

over the years." He gave Margeaux a knowing look, and she knew exactly what he was suggesting. "But we've called a truce. I'll never be his favorite person in the world. In fact, he could be the lone Council member who stands between me and my goal of joining the Crown Council one day. But we're working out our issues. I'm proving myself worthy."

Wow. Henri has designs on the Crown Council?

She never would've guessed that with a thousand chances. Not that he wasn't worthy. He was smart; he had a social conscience and he was charismatic. All of the qualities she lacked. Her father had been very vocal about how desperately he hoped Henri's good qualities would rub off on her.

That was one of the problems that eventually led to the blow up. She wasn't book smart. After her mother's death, she'd been so starved for normalcy and love that all she wanted to do was lash out—and make out with Henri. To somehow feel loved again. To make her world whole.

Of course things had changed over the years. Obviously, they had a lot of catching up to do.

As the group began their procession to the casino, Margeaux was well aware that Sydney trailed behind them like an afterthought. Her friends had snared Sydney, asking her questions, detaining her so that Margeaux and Henri could have the brief walk to the bar.

When her cell phone rang, Margeaux was making a mental note to give each of them a hug for always knowing exactly what to do at the right moment.

She didn't recognize the number and almost let it go to voice mail, but something made her pick up.

"Ms. Broussard, this is Aretha Garibaldi, I'm one of your father's nurses at St. Michel General Hospital. I am so sorry to be the bearer of unpleasant news, but your father has taken a turn for the worse. Could you please come right away?"

Chapter Three

The seventeenth-century Broussard manor house was set back from the road fifty yards, and shielded by a rustic, nine-foot stone wall that was overgrown with ivy and climbing roses that bloomed all year, thanks to St. Michel's mild climate.

As Henri steered his BMW up the winding gravel driveway, Margeaux kept her face turned toward the window.

"How can he be dead?" Her words were a whisper, barely audible over the crunch of

tires on gravel. "He told me he was going to be released from the hospital tomorrow."

Henri reached out and took Margeaux's hand. She turned her palm so that her fingers laced through his and held on like he was her lifeline.

After the call, Henri had given Sydney money for a taxi and had driven Margeaux to the hospital.

Colbert was still alive when they'd arrived. He'd lasted long enough to gasp a labored "It's fine. Everything is fine. Henri will know what to do. Follow his instructions and all will be fine."

The worst part was Henri had no idea what the man was talking about. They'd barely been on speaking terms, only beginning to mend their differences over the past couple of months.

Had he somehow known his time on earth was limited?

Colbert was renowned for holding grudges. Henri couldn't blame him for the one he held against him. But when it came down to it, that didn't mean Henri liked it.

In late summer the year he and Margeaux

were both sixteen, the press had snapped photos of Henri and Margeaux as they'd skinny dipped in the lake behind their houses. The headline *Europe's Worst Father Lets Daughter Run Wild Because He's Too Busy Playing Politics* may have lambasted Crown Council member Colbert Broussard, but it had caused scandal for both families.

The thing that hurt the most was that the scumbag reporter had actually hit the nail on the head. Never before had a tabloid headline packed so much truth.

But that's not how newly widowed Colbert saw it. Margeaux was the problem. She'd been failing at school, staying out until all hours of the morning, and now this very public embarrassment. It was the last straw. He decided he couldn't handle Margeaux and made plans to send her to boarding school in France. When Henri had refused to run away with her, she'd cut all ties—with her father and him—and had done her best to live up to the wild-child image that had caused her father to send her away.

Colbert had blamed Henri as much as he'd blamed Margeaux, and even years later he had gone to great lengths to make life difficult for

Henri. Colbert was the lone Crown Council Member who had opposed Henri's appointment as Minister of Arts and Education—it had taken an override from the king for Henri to get the job; and Colbert remained the voice against Henri's consideration as a serious candidate for future Crown Council appointment—a position that would take years to land.

When Henri had returned to his family home next door to Broussard after purchasing the property from his father's estate, Colbert had ignored him. The homes were large, with an orchard between them. So it was easy to avoid each other. Henri respected the old man's wishes.

That's why it had thrown Henri when Colbert contacted him about a state matter two months ago; he'd begun reaching out about business matters but said nothing about "instructions" for Margeaux; for that matter, he hadn't even mentioned Margeaux.

Perhaps all he meant was that Henri would help Margeaux with the memorial arrangements.

But that didn't amount to much.

The hospital had instructions that Colbert's

body was to be cremated. More instructions would follow.

In the meantime, Henri and Margeaux's friends helped her settle into her father's house.

Walking into her father's house was like going back in time. Everything was exactly as she remembered it, including her bedroom with the blue walls, white iron bed frame and the poster of Maxfield Parrish's *Sleeping Beauty*.

In a sense, she felt like Sleeping Beauty awakening from a long slumber, or, given her father's death, perhaps it was more apt to say she was stuck in a nightmare.

His death was like being blindsided by an eighteen-wheeler. They'd been rolling along, making better progress than she'd ever imagined in the twenty minutes she had to spend with him.

All those years they'd wasted only to reunite for a fraction of an hour. But at least their last minutes were amiable.

His nurse had explained that her father was sicker than he'd let on; she said those who were

terminal had more control over when they went than most people realized.

Terminal?

She had no idea he was *that* sick. He'd promised her that everything would be "fine" and that he'd be leaving the hospital….

She never dreamed it would be *this* way.

He'd said for her to follow Henri's lead, but both she and Henri were at a loss about how to interpret that until two days later, when the two of them met with her father's attorney.

She and the girls had been getting ready for dinner. A.J., who was a chef, was in the kitchen preparing it, while Pepper and Caroline were starting a fire in the old mosaic-covered, outdoor fireplace and setting the old stone trestle table out in the rose garden.

It was unseasonably warm for November. Even though the weather in St. Michel remained temperate all year, this particular evening, they were experiencing clear skies and highs in the upper sixties. Perfect weather for dinner al fresco.

Margeaux was both unnerved by the news that the attorney might bring and soothed by seeing Henri at the door.

"Margeaux, this is your father's solicitor, Pascal Moreau," said Henri.

Pascal was a slight, balding man. He had a serious demeanor, but he was quick to look her in the eye and offer a firm handshake.

"Come in," she said.

"Something smells good," said Henri.

"The girls and I are fixing a feast."

"I'm sorry to disturb your dinner preparations," said Pascal.

"Then stay for dinner," A.J. called from the kitchen. "There's plenty."

"Hi, A.J., that sounds great," Henri answered. "It smells wonderful and I'm starved. But do you mind if we borrow Margeaux for a moment? We have some business to discuss."

Margeaux glanced at the large envelope in his hands.

"This is from my father?" she asked.

Pascal nodded.

She ignored the chill that danced over her. Henri and Pascal were bringing answers—or at least giving her the means for closure.

Her friends had been wonderful to change their plans and move into the house with her. But they couldn't stay here forever. Margeaux

wanted to be on course doing right by her father before they left.

She led Henri and Pascal into the room that had been her father's first floor study. Even though Margeaux had never been close to her father, it was there that she felt his presence most. There was so much of him in that room: a wool sweater was draped across the back of his leather desk chair, the seat of which gave in certain places, molded by his shape and weight. A notepad lay open with his writing scrawled across it. A brass letter opener rested on top of a stack of bills and correspondence. His pipe, with teeth marks on the stem and a half-full pouch of tobacco, sat next to the small Tiffany desk lamp. It was a working desk, but it was tidy and all business, just like him.

That's why she wanted her father's will to be read in here.

Even though she'd reacquainted herself with every room in the house, she still wasn't completely comfortable in here. As a child she'd never been allowed to cross the threshold. When her father was inside with the doors shut, it meant he was not to be disturbed.

Maybe it was part defiance; maybe it was a

last ditch effort to connect with him, because here, out of any room in the house, was where her father's spirit seemed to linger.

His presence was still all so fresh, as if he'd be coming back to tend to business any moment.

"Are you okay?" Henri asked.

He touched her cheek with the back of his hand and the intimacy startled her.

"Yes." She walked to the window and opened the shutters. The last strands of twilight shone in. She shivered again and swallowed her sadness, deliberately focusing her gaze on Henri.

His handsome face was her sanctuary. Staring at him in the half light, she wanted to go to him, bury her face in his neck and lose herself in the achingly familiar scent of him, draw strength from the warm shelter of his arms.

"Are you sure?" he asked.

Yes.

"We don't have to do this now," Monsieur Pascal offered. "Traditionally, we wait until after the funeral or memorial service to handle such delicate matters as this." He gestured to the envelope. "For reasons your father did not

share, he requested that this matter be taken care of before the funeral. But we're not legally bound to proceed that way. If you'd like to delay, we can make another appointment."

She blinked, smiled apologetically at Pascal and swallowed the lump that had settled in her throat. "Now is as good a time as any."

She gestured to the overstuffed armchair. Pascal settled himself and began pulling papers from the envelope. She and Henri took a seat on the sofa and waited for him to begin.

"This is your father's last will and testament," he said. "I worked with him on it in the days after he first fell ill, but I believe he was of sound mind and it is something he seems to have put a lot of thought into."

Pascal fanned through the pages, finally letting the stack fall to a rest in his lap. He looked perplexed.

"What he wants is kind of complicated. Do you want to read through it or do you want me to tell you?"

Right. Even on a good day her dyslexia would make it difficult to read and comprehend the legalese. As nervous as she was right

now, if she attempted to read it herself they'd be here all night.

She shrugged off the feelings of stupidity that were trying to envelop her. "Now you're making me nervous," she said to Pascal. "Please, just tell me what he has to say."

The attorney nodded. "I'll read it to you."

"Dear Margeaux,

"I realize we've had our differences, but if you are reading this, it means you at least made an attempt at reconciliation with me, and therefore I felt there had been significant growth on your part before I departed this earth. If not, my entire estate would have been auctioned and the proceeds would have gone to worthy charities, but since you are hearing this, it means my estate will transfer to you upon completion of tasks that will be outlined in a moment.

"In my old age, I realized as your father there were many lessons that were my responsibility to teach you. Because I neglected to do so, I admit that our estrangement is not entirely your fault."

Henri took her hand. "Are you okay?"

The truth was she was numb, except for the warmth of her hand in his. *Lessons?* He was shouldering part of the blame? If she thought about it too hard she would break down. So, instead, she nodded. "Go ahead."

"I realize you're making your own way in the world. You seem to have toned down your ways and I understand you have a job and a life in Texas. Don't be surprised. I've had people checking on you."

Pascal glanced up, this time as if to gauge her reaction or maybe it was because it was getting dark in the room and he needed more light to read. Margeaux reached over and turned on the lamp on the end table.

Pascal squinted at the light and continued.

"We cannot undo the past, but we can learn from it. So it is in that spirit that I am sending you on a scavenger hunt, of sorts, so that you will become better acquainted with your heritage. My rep-

resentative will inform you of the details in a moment.

"I realize these tasks will take some time and will disrupt your life, but if you will see it through to the end, there will be a greater reward than I can explain here and now. You simply must experience it.

"To Henri Lejardin, you and my daughter, Margeaux, were once close. I will depend on you to help her through this journey. To be with her every step of the way. If you do, there will be something for you in the end, too.

"However, should either of you refuse, you will forfeit your portion of the reward.

With love and regards,

Your father"

They were silent for a moment.

Margeaux wasn't sure what threw her most— this crash course in the Broussard family history that her father was trying to thrust upon her, or the fact that he'd signed his letter *with love and regards*.

Love and regards.

Love and regards?

On one hand, they seemed to cancel each other out—you either sent love or regards. Love was a hug, the other was a handshake. But she couldn't recall a time when she remembered her father ever uttering the word *love*.

She could be cynical or she could claim this love he was offering, despite it being sandwiched between *with* and *regards*.

"What the heck is he talking about?" she finally asked.

Henri squeezed her hand, and Pascal flipped to the next page without looking at her.

"He wants you to visit the Saint Mary of the Universe Orphanage near Avignon and the Saint James convent about ten miles from there. He wants you to spend a week in each place. Details are to unfold as your journey progresses. Will you accept this challenge?"

"What?" Margeaux shifted, hating the confusion she felt. It made her feel dumb and when she felt this way, her gut reaction was to run. It didn't make sense, and she wondered if she'd missed something.

Pascal must have read her concerns because

he said, "I know it doesn't make sense now, but your father seemed to think that if you would take the time to visit these places his reasons would be self-explanatory."

The first boarding school her father had sent her to was near Avignon. She had no desire to go back.

"Why now?"

Pascal smiled, but it looked conciliatory. "He says specific instructions will be delivered after you make the decision to accept or decline the tasks. But I am allowed to give you some information on Saint Mary of the Universe Orphanage. Here it is."

He handed her an envelope. She opened it and glanced through the information for clues. The words seemed to jump around, but she focused hard on the first page, which looked like basic information about Saint Mary's.

She'd read it later, once she had time to focus and digest the information and the odd journey her father was thrusting upon her from the grave. Was he trying to preach the lesson that someone always has it worse?

Henri placed his other hand over hers. "Are you okay?"

"I will be."

Couldn't her father at least give her most recent wounds from losing him a chance to heal before he asserted his power?

"There are two last things," Pascal looked apologetic. "He stipulates if you don't comply, the estate will be sold and split between the institutions your father wants you to visit, and if you do comply, then you must complete your visits within three months of today. Will you accept the terms of his challenge and if so, when would you like to visit?"

Despite the amazing savory aromas that were filling the house, Pascal declined the invitation to dinner, but Henri stayed. As he followed Margeaux out to the kitchen to help A.J. with preparations, he felt guilty.

Colbert's baiting rankled him. Although he had no idea what this *reward* would be, he wouldn't take a penny of the estate from Margeaux if she decided she wanted to see this charade through to the end.

The only reason he'd go through with it was to help her with what was sure to be an emotionally challenging escapade.

What the hell was Colbert thinking, asking him to lead Margeaux to an orphanage and convent in the south of France? What did the man have up his sleeve?

He was a piece of work—dictating people's actions even from the grave.

He wanted the chance to talk to Margeaux about it—to tell her it was not his intention to horn in on her inheritance, but dinner preparations were coming together and A.J. handed him a head of romaine, asking him to wash and chop it for salads.

The methodical work was good for sorting out his thoughts, so Henri complied. As he was standing at the sink washing the lettuce, through the kitchen window he noticed Sydney's car drive up the long gravel driveway and park in front of the house.

What was she doing here? She hadn't mentioned anything about stopping by.

"Are you expecting anyone?" he asked, fully expecting A.J. to say no.

"Oh, yeah, Sydney's joining us."

"Really?" he said as he watched her get out of her car and navigate the front steps to the

front door. "How did she secure an invitation for herself?"

A.J. threw him a strange look. "We invited her. She called earlier today saying she wanted to come by and pay her respects to Margeaux. You know, bring her some flowers. Cheer her up. That's what friends do."

Friends?

Since when were Sydney and Margeaux friends?

The thought made him uncomfortable.

He heard one of the women call, "I'll get it," in response to the knock on the door. Then he heard muffled greetings, undefined but happy feminine notes that drifted from the foyer to the kitchen, straight to his nerves.

Sydney wasn't the type who collected girl-friends unless she had a reason. His gut was telling him she was here tonight on a reconnaissance mission.

He heard Margeaux greet Sydney before they made their way into the kitchen. And when Sydney, who was holding a bottle of wine and a box of chocolates from Maya's Chocolate Shop—a St. Michel institution—saw Henri standing at the sink holing the head of romaine,

the surprise that flashed in her eyes confirmed his suspicions.

"Fancy seeing you here," she said to Henri, her British accent sounding clipped. "I didn't realize you were invited."

She flashed one of her dazzling smiles.

"Funny, I thought the same thing when I saw your car pull up the driveway." He gestured toward the kitchen window. "Though, I live next door, if you'll remember."

He winked, but it was meant to be more touché than flirty.

"Well, here we are." She turned to Margeaux. "How may I help with dinner?"

As she arranged the beautiful bunch of mixed flowers that Sydney had brought, Margeaux noticed the tension between Sydney and Henri. It was palpable enough to slice with a butter knife.

Still, even as rattled by Henri's presence as Sydney seemed, she was overly nice to Margeaux. For some strange reason, her attention made Margeaux uncomfortable. What was going on?

The woman was gorgeous—tall and dark

with smart, emerald-green eyes. Dressed in classic black slacks and a cashmere twin set, she was the epitome of elegance. The night Margeaux met her, she'd been achingly positive Sydney was in love with Henri, but now, she wasn't so sure.

Still, the old, less evolved Margeaux wanted to claim Henri to herself. To tease him and tempt him and see if the spark from the past was still alive and well. But the new, more level-headed Margeaux realized she'd been away for a long time. Of course Henri would move on with his life. He deserved someone like Sydney.

Still, every nerve in her body objected to the thought of losing him forever. All it took was one glance, one brush of his hand and she threatened to spontaneously combust. The problem was, they'd been apart for years and he had Sydney in his life—whatever the nature of their relationship might be. Margeaux certainly didn't want to get in the middle of it, or the low-toned, private conversation Sydney and Henri were having by the far counter as they worked together making the salad.

Rather than torment herself by watching

them, Margeaux grabbed a crystal platter and the box of Maya's chocolates and went to the terrace. There she tried to re-focus as she arranged the dessert and made sure the table was ready for the tarragon chicken, green beans, salad and fresh baked bread A.J. had prepared.

The table looked better than if Martha Stewart had popped in for a surprise visit. Pepper was putting on the finishing touches by lighting votive candles she'd managed to find. She'd worked her magic, drawing from the abundance of fruit from the orchard and fall foliage that adorned the garden.

"You could probably create a tablescape out of rags and clothespins, couldn't you?" Margeaux teased.

Pepper blew out a match and pulled a face as if she were contemplating the design problem. "I'll have to give that a try sometime."

"I'm sure you probably could make it happen," Margeaux said. "Tonight, everything looks exquisite."

Just then, Caroline carried out six wine-glasses and a bottle each of merlot and chilled chardonnay.

She held up the bottles for Margeaux and Pepper to choose, then handed Margeaux a glass of red, and Pepper a glass of white.

On her terrace, surrounded by her friends, Margeaux noticed that the vibe was different than in the kitchen. It felt good, and she was filled with gratitude for the blessing of her girlfriends, but there was that stab of regret reminding her that, thanks to her father's *lesson plan,* she'd be away from them for God knew how long.

She'd be with Henri, which set her stomach spiraling. But she reined it in. Who knew if he would put his job aside to join her on these adventures? If they did travel together, what would she do about their undeniable chemistry? They couldn't simply be friends.

She shook off the thought because she had more important things to worry about—such as how she hadn't told her girls about her father's plans for her. Not yet. There were still a few days left before they had to leave. She'd wait until the time was right.

The three were toasting each other when Sydney joined them with a tray of bread and plated salads.

"Where in Texas are each of you from?" she asked.

"Austin," Caroline answered, offering her a glass of wine. She chose the chardonnay.

"I *love* Texas," Sydney said, and proceeded to ask questions about the weather, the economy, the housing market. The men.

The men?

"Why are you so interested?" asked Pepper. "I mean, what about Henri?"

Margeaux shot Pepper a dagger of a sideways glance for bringing up the big elephant in the room, even though the same question had been burning in the back of her own throat, too. That was the thing about Pepper—she said what everyone else was thinking. With her sweet accent and proper debutante polishing, she could get away with what most people couldn't.

But that's when Margeaux realized Sydney was looking at *her*. "I have no idea," Sydney said. "I think Henri's the one who isn't quite sure what he wants."

An uncomfortable silence settled over the women, as unwelcome as a sudden rise in the humidity. Margeaux felt heat burn in her

décolletage and creep its way up her neck, settling on her cheeks.

"Oh, well, then," Pepper said, filling the silence. "I'm just saying, Texas is a great place, but it's certainly not Europe."

More uncomfortable silence.

"Oh, my goodness," Pepper exclaimed. "Caroline, do you realize we haven't even offered our chef and sous chef glasses of wine? That is a high-grade problem, and we should tend to it immediately."

"Absolutely, I'll help you," said Caroline.

They disappeared into the house like twin Bacchuses on the lamb, leaving Margeaux alone with Sydney.

"Are you considering a move to Texas?" Margeaux asked, simply for the sake of making conversation.

Sydney seemed to weigh the question for a moment. "May I trust you with a secret?" she asked, lowering her voice in a conspiratorial fashion that made Margeaux even more uncomfortable.

"Sure," said Margeaux.

Neither smiling nor frowning, Sydney pinned Margeaux with her emerald gaze. Margeaux

felt as if she were being sized up. "I'm seriously considering a move to the Dallas area."

Sydney wasn't *trusting* her. She was testing her.

"Really?" Margeaux sipped her wine. "Why would you do that when your job is still in St. Michel?"

Sydney smiled, but the expression was somehow sad. "I've never seen him look at anyone the way he looks at you."

Oh, no. Margeaux flinched. She crossed to the table and started opening another bottle of wine. Pepper and Caroline had taken the open bottles inside, and with the direction this conversation was taking, Margeaux definitely needed some liquid courage.

The question was obviously rhetorical because Sydney didn't wait for an answer. "You realize he's still in love with you, don't you? I saw it from the second he set sight on you again at the casino after all these years."

Chapter Four

After Sydney said good-night, Henri stayed to assist with the cleanup, hoping for a chance to talk more with Margeaux about the news Pascal had delivered. However, Caroline, A.J. and Pepper refused to let Margeaux and Henri help. Instead, they shooed the couple out to the terrace to enjoy the last of the fire and the wine.

"We've got this under control," insisted A.J.

"I'm sure you do," Henri replied, "but isn't there a rule about the cook not cleaning

up since she did all the work to prepare the meal?"

"Cooking's the fun part," Pepper said, the wine rounding her words even more. "Seriously, we don't mind a bit."

With that, she handed each of them a clean wineglass and closed the French doors between the terrace and the patio, shutting Margeaux and Henri out in their own little moonlit world.

Though he'd been willing to help, Henri was glad for the time alone with Margeaux. The evening had been filled with lively conversation, but she'd been a little subdued after Pascal's visit. The blues that had settled around her since her father's death seemed a bit more pronounced tonight, despite the good friends who were rallying around her.

A full moon and the low, red glow of the fire lit the terrace. Henri noticed Margeaux shiver and rub her arms with her hands. She was wearing faded blue jeans and a long-sleeved light pink cashmere sweater that looked so soft it begged to be touched, but the temperature was falling fast and he knew the sweater wasn't heavy enough to keep her warm.

"Are you cold?"

She nodded. "Just a little."

"Here, take my jacket." He slid out of the coat and slipped it around her shoulders. Then he took her hand and led her to the fire.

Margeaux settled herself on a wicker love-seat in front of the fire as Henri emptied the last of the red wine into their glasses, picked up the platter of Maya's chocolate and joined her on the cushion-covered couch. Their knees grazed when he sat down, but neither pulled away.

Henri offered her a piece of chocolate. She took one and bit into it, letting the delectable silkiness of it melt over her tongue. She tasted hints of cinnamon, spices and rose petals mixed into the deep, rich cocoa.

Henri did the same, and held her gaze as they clinked wineglasses.

For a moment, they sat in companionable silence, enjoying the chocolate, sipping the wine and relaxing in the warm glow of the fire.

Henri cleared his throat and ran a hand through his hair. He seemed a little nervous. She wondered if the setting was a little too

intimate for him. Perhaps he felt as if he were being untrue to Sydney?

She scooted away, allowing for some extra space between them. "What are you thinking?" she asked.

"I just want you to know," he said, staring into his wineglass. "I don't have any designs on your father's estate. Despite this task he's asking us to complete, I believe everything should go to you."

Ah, he *was* uncomfortable. This was his way of telling her he couldn't go away with her for two weeks in Avignon. She'd told Pascal she would do it. She'd made arrangements to be in St. Michel with her father for the foreseeable future. Now that she'd had a couple of hours to digest the "challenge," as her father had put it, she was curious, and she had the time. But how could she expect Henri to clear his schedule for her?

"Henri, don't worry about it. I know my father's little game is an inconvenience. I'd never expect you to drop everything to do it."

He shook his head. "No, that's not what I meant. I fully intend to help you through this, just as your father asked. I just don't want you

to misunderstand and think that I want something in return."

*Okay...hmmm...*now she was even more
confused.

"Don't you think Sydney will mind you
going away with me?"

"Why would she mind?"

"Well...I just thought... She left early tonight, didn't she?" Margeaux stared at the
flames because she was too afraid to look at
him.

"Actually, I was surprised to see her here
tonight."

"She's a persistent woman, isn't she? She
seems to get what she wants."

"What do you mean?"

Margeaux looked up and seemed to assess
him for a moment. The firelight made her blue
eyes shimmer. Yet, there was a note of sadness
in her expression that made him long to reach
out and pull her close, to assure her that everything would be okay. Even though he couldn't
guarantee that, he silently vowed to be by her
side every step of the way during this scavenger
hunt her father was putting her through.

She cleared her throat. "What do I mean?"

she repeated his question, obviously buying time.

He nodded.

"I guess I'm trying to figure out what she means to you."

"And that makes *her* a persistent woman, huh?" He wanted to make her laugh, but she didn't, and now it seemed as if he were the one buying time. "I'm not sure what you're asking."

She shifted and her knee pulled away from his.

"I think you know exactly what I'm asking. But if you want me to spell it out for you, I need to know if you two are...*involved*."

There was something exhilarating about her curiosity, about the fact that she cared.

"Sydney is a wonderful woman," he said, "and I wouldn't be telling the truth if I didn't tell you that for a while we've walked the line between friendship and..." And what? People didn't waver between love and friendship. Two people were either in love or they weren't. If you had to think about it, wasn't that pretty telling? "And I guess with her I never discovered what was on the other side of friendship."

Margeaux squinted up at him for a long time, as if trying to measure his honesty. "But she seems to want a lot more than...*friendship*."

Henri shrugged, not really wanting to dissect his relationship with Sydney. In fact, he didn't want to talk about Sydney at all. Then, for a moment he thought he glimpsed something familiar in Margeaux's eyes—a look that hinted at the past; one that stirred old feelings.

"Friendship is all I've been able to offer her. And I think it's all I'll ever have for her. I let you go because I had to," he said. "It was what you wanted. But I never stopped loving you. I feel as though I let you down. I know I should have come after you, but you shut me out."

"When I left, I shut everything and everyone out," she said.

"Why?"

"Because it was the only way I could function."

Looking at him now, it all seemed so simple. Why had it seemed so hard back then? What was difficult was fighting the compulsion to blame herself as she thought of all the things she should've done instead of shutting him out—fighting the bitterness that always crept

up when she thought of the way her father had shut her out. Still, she wished she hadn't made so many mistakes, lost so much time.

There were so many things she had not told Henri. Important things she should have shared, but back then she'd had a hard time forming the words on even the night that she'd asked him to run away had started out all wrong. To go away so that she wouldn't have to go to boarding school.

Henri had said no.

And before she could tell him *why* they needed to go away together, he did something so unexpected, something so far from anything she'd ever imagined—he'd told her that her going away was for the best, and that since she'd be gone, it was best that they break up.

No.

He belonged to her; they belonged to each other. There could never be anyone else.

Margeaux had been so floored that she couldn't speak. All her words bottled up inside.

First her father had rejected her.

Now Henri. The one person she thought would love her forever.

But Henri wanted out.

Being here with him now, after all these years, she wondered if she should tell him what she should have told him all those years ago, but so much time had passed and really, there was no reason to bring it up now.

Especially when he reached forward to touch her face, then stopped before he did.

"What?" he asked. "You look like you want to say something."

She shook her head. Her skin tingled with want for him and she shifted closer. He pulled her into him, and as he caressed her back, she melted at the feel of his hands on her. Until this moment, she hadn't realized just how much she'd missed his touch.

How much she missed him. No, now that everything was brand new, there was no use in rehashing the past. Especially since it wouldn't change anything. But they could move forward.

He felt achingly familiar and brand-new all at once. Even though secrets of the past niggled at her to pull away, to talk to him, self-preservation looked after the scared, lonely teenage girl in her—the part of her that wanted

to disappear into the sanctuary of his strong, familiar arms, to fall head-over-heels into a place where life made sense and she didn't have to worry about proving herself or being proper or being judged.

His breath was hot on her temple. And hers was ragged as she sighed. Then his lips skimmed her cheek, and Margeaux tilted back her head, looking up at him. His eyes were hungry and hooded and the next thing she knew his lips were brushing hers.

The kiss started slow and soft, then ignited into ravenous greed that had her parting her lips so he could deepen the kiss, fisting her hands into the cotton of his shirt, leaning into him as if her next breath would come from him.

For a moment, the whole world disappeared. Until he pulled her tighter, staking his claim, unspoken feelings pouring out in this wordless confession.

He tasted like red wine, chocolate, cinnamon and something exotic. That familiar hint of yesteryear, mixed with the promise of now.

A moment ago she was worried that he might have feelings for another woman, and

now he was kissing her so thoroughly she had no doubt of his loyalty. Feelings inside her that had stirred when she'd seen him in the casino were awakening, blossoming into a passion that threatened to consume her.

She forgot the once logical rationale for protecting her heart. Or maybe she no longer cared. The reasons began to shift and span the gap of years until it bridged the present with the past.

Margeaux had no idea how much time had passed as they held and kissed each other. It was even better than she remembered. Because they were no longer kids, hiding out, stealing moments. This was Henri, holding her close, kissing her lips, rendering the years they'd been apart irrelevant.

"There is so much between us we left undone." He rested his forehead against hers, his lips a whisper away. "What are we going to do about that?"

That was the burning question.

She knew what she wanted in the here and now, but she still didn't know how much of that undone past she should dredge up.

* * *

Colbert's funeral was larger and better attended than she'd expected. Her father's body had lain in state in the seventeenth-century chapel on the palace grounds and was transported to the ornate St. Michel Cathedral.

Carabineers lined the path from the palace chapel to the garden's Gate of Honor. The soldiers in red military dress uniforms wore bronze helmets with black plumes that trembled slightly in the cool November breeze. They played trumpet fanfares and beat drums covered with black cloth.

Colbert's coffin was draped with the St. Michel flag. Clad in a black dress with a black veil, Margeaux held Henri's hand as they walked behind the casket. Even though it wasn't traditional for the Queen of St. Michel to walk in the funeral procession, Margeaux was touched when Queen Sophie, who was married to Henri's brother Luc, reached out to her in support. Sophie, Luc and Henri's other brother Alex and his wife, Julianne, along with Margeaux's girlfriends and other members of the Crown Council formed the procession, escorting her to the limousines waiting to transport

them to the St. Michel Cathedral where her father would be buried.

As the Gate of Honor was symbolically closed after Colbert's casket was carried out, Margeaux's heart overflowed with bittersweet appreciation; her father was well respected and she was welcome in St. Michel despite her sixteen-year absence.

The procession drove from the palace, past hundreds of somberly dressed St. Michel residents, to the ancient St. Michel Cathedral.

The cathedral was filled to standing room, with dignitaries and heads of state from all over the world; Europe's royals, nobles, and VIPs rounded out the cast that came to bid farewell to one of Europe's most respected political figures. Everyone was dressed almost uniformly in black, as they waited in the cathedral for the funeral procession.

Heads bowed as his coffin was carried up the aisle; once it reached its destination at the front a sword was placed atop.

Opening the service, the officiating Archbishop said, "Colbert Broussard, beloved son and servant of St. Michel, loving and loved

father of Margeaux, now joins his late wife, Bernadette, to rest in death's peaceful sleep."

The words *loving and loved father* sliced through the haze of Margeaux's grief and a tear meandered down her cheek. She had a choice—she could wallow in the past and weigh herself down with things that were too late to change or she could push beyond.

Loving and loved father.

The words made her feel claustrophobic and for a brief spell she wrestled with the over-whelming urge to get up and run out of the church. She pulled her hand from Henri's and scooted forward.

Loving and loved father.

Then Henri slid his arm along the back of the church pew, settling it on her shoulder, pull-ing her close. Margeaux collapsed into him. He kissed the top of her head and her mind found comfort in the memory of his kiss the night of Pascal's reading of the will.

So much wasted time.

Why had she waited so long to come home? If she'd known her father would've been so receptive she would've reached out long ago. But maybe she wasn't ready—maybe neither of

them would've been. Their brief time together felt unfinished.

She'd never lived up to his expectations— she'd been a disappointment to him. The stupid, wild child—the *fille sauvage* who was more of an embarrassment than he could handle.

Of all the regrets, she wished she would have had the opportunity to prove to him that she wasn't a brainless failure. In fact, she was smart enough to get by, to cover up her dyslexia—even though, at the time, she had no idea that's what plagued her—disguising it by pretending not to care about academics. By being footloose, wild and free.

Of course, as far as her father was concerned, the wild streak factored down to silliness, and silly girls were stupid girls, whose place it was to be quiet and not draw attention to themselves since they had nothing intelligent to offer.

Margeaux hated this label, hated being expected to be the pretty girl who was barely seen and never heard. So she'd made sure he not only saw her but heard the noise she created.

Her wild behavior had come from a basic desire to be loved, flaws and all.

Her father was gone and he would never

know this. They would never have the relationship she'd desperately wanted, even when she'd done everything in her power to anger him and ultimately send her away.

This above all else wracked her with grief.

Margeaux leaned into Henri, taking the hand that caressed her arm, clinging to him for dear life.

Somehow, she made it through the service. Colbert would be buried beside Bernadette. A plain slab of marble beside his wife's resting place in the cemetery had been engraved with his name. Another detail Henri had helped Margeaux arrange.

They emerged from the church into the bright, sunny afternoon. The air was crisp and cool; the sky was clear and bright blue, incongruent with the dark, burning hole yawning in Margeaux's heart.

As she and Henri began the walk from the grave to the waiting limo, Henri was talking to his brother Alex about plans for the post-funeral reception. That's when a thin, disheveled-looking man in a wrinkled suit with a necktie that was haphazardly hung about two

inches below his unbuttoned collar approached Margeaux.

"Pardon me, Ms. Broussard. May I have a word?"

Margeaux stopped and turned to him. There was something about the fellow's pock-marked, sunken cheeks and unpolished British accent that tweaked a memory. But she couldn't place him.

"Yes?" she responded, pushing back her hat's black lace veil to get a better look at him.

"Terribly sorry for your loss," he said.

"Thank you." *Who was he?*

"You've been away from St. Michel for a long time. Are you back for good now?"

She didn't quite know how to answer the question. "I have some personal matters to take care of while I'm here, but— Excuse me, but do I know you?"

From his pocket, the man pulled a small camera and clicked photo after photo. "Rory Malone, *Daily Mail*."

Oh, no! She gasped.

Hearing the name was a kick in the gut. This was the reporter who had been responsible for the skinny-dipping photographs of Henri and

Margeaux, and the story about Colbert being such a bad father.

Even though he looked older and harder, she'd never forget that name. The jerk was up to his old tricks. Even on this day that should have been sacred.

"Would you care to elaborate on these personal matters?" he said, sliding the wristband of his camera over his hand and producing a small notebook and pen from his coat pocket.

"No, go away, please. The Crown Council public information officer can give you all the information you'll need for a story about my father's funeral."

Henri stepped between Margeaux and Malone. "Please have some respect. Leave her alone."

"Henri Lejardin," said Malone. "Are you and Ms. Broussard involved again?"

Henri rounded on the creep. "If you have one shred of decency in your hollow soul, you'll go away and leave her alone."

Henri put a protective arm around Margeaux and walked her to the waiting car. Undeterred, the jerk trailed along behind.

"Ms. Broussard, were you pregnant when you left St. Michel sixteen years ago?"

Margeaux heard the deafening silence in the surrounding crowd as she let Henri lead her away.

"Did you have a child with Margeaux?" Sydney feigned a scandalized surprise. She stood in the doorway of Henri's office holding a copy of the *Daily Mail* open to the page where the small article was buried, smirking at the obvious absurdity of the trash.

"Sydney, don't."

It wasn't true, and Henri refused to even joke about it.

The impudent nature of the article—the fact that the weasel had disrespected not only Margeaux, but the entire principality of St. Michel after the funeral of one of its highest ranking dignitaries—left such a bad taste in his mouth, he hoped he never saw the little rat again. Because he couldn't guarantee the sewer dweller would survive with a full set of teeth.

"Come on, Henri, lighten up," she teased. "I'm just treating it like the joke it is."

Henri frowned at her.

"Well, that's almost as inappropriate as the story," he said. "It's nothing to laugh about. But just for the record, Margeaux wasn't pregnant when she left and we don't have a child. Anything else you'd like to know?"

Sydney had been scarce for the better part of the week surrounding Colbert's funeral. In fact, he hadn't seen her since the dinner at Margeaux's house.

He thought she was giving them room so that they could make all the arrangements for Colbert and get past the burial, but come to think of it, he wasn't even sure if she'd been at the funeral. As an employee of the state, she would have been welcome at the service, of course. In fact, he was surprised she hadn't been right in the thick of things given that the Queen was there. Since they'd been dating, she'd been pushing for an introduction. Because of her over-eagerness and the fact that he wasn't certain how he felt about her, he'd held off.

Now he was glad he'd listened to his gut.

"I'm sorry," she said. "I certainly don't mean to be inappropriate. Do you have a moment?

There's something important we need to talk about."

He nodded. He had a feeling they were about to have one of those where-do-we-stand talks. Sydney was a fine woman. She deserved someone who loved her with his entire heart. He'd never been able to make that jump from dating to exclusive commitment with Sydney. Though he didn't want to hurt her, he was still in love with Margeaux. It was time he told her.

She closed the door, took a seat in one of the chairs in front of his desk. She crossed her legs primly at the ankle, rather than going for the maneuver where she crossed one leg over the other for maximum skirt-hiking affect.

Good. This was going to be a serious conversation rather than a battle of flirtatious quips.

"Despite the recent chaos," she said, "the museum staff and I managed to get the catalogue printed and the show open."

"Yes, you and your staff did a great job. I apologize for not having commended you sooner."

She waved away his apology.

Patrons, the Crown Council and the general public deemed the show a success. In fact, it

was a welcome bright spot to offset the loss of Colbert Broussard. Henri had considered delaying the opening, but the Council had unanimously agreed Colbert would want the show to go on.

So it did: a memoriam to him.

"Well, there is one way that you can make it up to me if you feel *that* badly." She arched her left brow, and Henri opened his mouth to turn the conversation away from the road he was sure she was going to digress.

But Sydney held up her hand. "No, wait, please, Henri. This isn't easy for me to do. So, let me finish."

She swallowed and he could see her throat work as she did.

"I've been offered another job—in Dallas, Texas, of all places—and I'd like to be released from my duties immediately."

It was the last thing Henri expected her to say.

She must have seen it in his face because she said, "At this point the show can run itself. My assistant is well versed in the day-to-day operations. And you have Margeaux. Please, Henri, let me go."

Chapter Five

The downtown square was abuzz with people. Margeaux, Pepper, A.J and Caroline had to sidestep shoppers juggling multiple bags, merchants sweeping their entryways, and artists painting at easels set up in the middle of the walkway.

As Caroline snapped a photo of a cat perched on the bakery's windowsill, she nearly tripped over a dog trolling for attention in front of the butcher shop.

St. Michel used to be a winter retreat for Britain's elite and famous. Now, the big season

was summer. So, even though the square was well populated, at least they could enjoy it without the traffic jams and other hassles of summer tourism.

"Mmm...do you smell that?" A.J. said.

Margeaux drew in a deep breath and was treated to the tantalizing aroma of chocolate mixed with a hint of cinnamon, vanilla and... something magical. The scent was so tempting it made her mouth water.

If she remembered right, Maya's Chocolate was just around the corner. It was the shop where Sydney had purchased the delicious chocolate she'd brought to dinner that night she came over. Maya's was a legend and after sampling her wares, the girls couldn't wait to go and purchase some to take home.

Pepper inhaled greedily.

"I can almost taste that chocolate. It has to be close by."

Her friends were leaving the next day, so Margeaux had decided they needed a day of shopping and sightseeing. Plus, she owed Pepper big. After her friend learned that Sydney was interested in moving to Dallas, Pepper saw an opportunity to *relocate* Margeaux's

competition and called her *daddy* and told him she had a friend who needed a job. He said any friend of Pepper's would be an asset to Texron, his billion-dollar corporation in Dallas, Texas, and hired her sight unseen. On one hand, it was good to know that Sydney was out of the picture—at least in St. Michel, and because Sydney had been so grateful for the job, she was sure to be Pepper's new best friend in Dallas.

On one hand, Margeaux was grateful, but on the other, she didn't want to have to remove women from Henri's life in order to be his number one. In fact, she didn't want to be his number one if there was a number two. But right now, Sydney was the least of her worries. She still had to tell Henri the truth—that she had been pregnant before her father sent her off to boarding school. Not even her father had known. So, she had no idea how that tabloid reporter, Rory Malone, had.

The thought of that vile man made her shudder. Henri hadn't said a word about Malone's story. He hadn't asked if it were true. Therefore, she had to believe he'd written it off as tabloid trash.

Now, she had to decide whether to tell him the truth or to leave it alone. Right now, she was leaning toward letting everything be. She'd always imagined that they would have had a son.

Yes, a boy, because she was living proof that daughters were too much trouble. Or at least she'd been. The boy would be about fifteen now. Every once in a while, she'd spy a tall teenage boy with dark curly hair and imagine for a fleeting moment that he was their son.

Of course, the fantasy ended as soon as the boy walked by. It was the most bittersweet way to torture herself, because she hadn't known if the baby was a boy or a girl.

She never would know.

She picked up the pace and led her friends around a tight corner that led them to a street that was more of an ancient alleyway than a road built for anything other than pedestrian traffic.

"Here it is," Pepper said, pointing upward toward a sign.

They gathered around a window that was adorned with white lace curtains and was brimming with tins and boxes tied with colorful

ribbon. Pyramids of chocolate were arranged on several glass-dome-covered stands. Chocolate-dipped fruit, bonbons, truffles and petit fours were set out in bountiful array on doily-covered trays.

It was a feast for the eyes that tempted Margeaux to press her nose against the glass. It was just like she remembered.

Maybe it was the allure of decadence, or perhaps just the promise of what they'd tasted the other night, but they were drawn to the shop like starving men were pulled to a buffet.

As Caroline held open the glass shop door and they filed in, a wind chime sounded. The sumptuous scent of chocolate tantalized their senses.

"Bonjour!" a lilting voice rang out.

"Bonjour," they answered in unison.

"You'll have to be our interpreter," A.J. whispered. "Can you handle it?"

"No problem." Margeaux had been amazed by how many people in St. Michel spoke English now. It was a good thing because her French was rusty from not enough practice. In fact, even Henri had commented on how little of her accent remained after sixteen years.

During the time she thought she'd never return to her home, Margeaux had purposely tried to lose all traces of her accent. Even during the time she spent in Europe, she'd tried to make herself as American as possible.

The four women glanced around the shop, taking in the molds decorating the walls, the gift baskets artfully arranged on glass shelving, the confectionary displayed in the old fashioned cases and on the marble wrap stand. Then a woman with a blaze of curly, fire-red hair and a demeanor that was nearly as vibrant stepped out from a back room.

"Hello," she said, again, this time in heavily accented English. "Good morning to you."

That was Maya. Margeaux would know her anywhere—even from the days when Maya's mother had run the shop and she'd simply been her apprentice.

Maya's broad smile was nearly as warm as the color of her hair. "Someone's in love. I can smell it as strong as a Don Juan rose in full bloom."

In the span of a heartbeat, Margeaux felt all eyes on her and a blush capable of melting all the chocolate in the shop crept up her throat.

Maya tilted her head to the side and furrowed her brow scanning the four women. Her gaze flickered past Margeaux, then snapped back.

"Congratulations, it's you," she said. "It's been a long time coming, hasn't it? But no fear, this time you will get it right. But you need to be truthful with him."

Margeaux froze, but Maya had already moved on. She was smiling apologetically at the others. "No worries, your turns will come in due time. Don't worry, everything will work out fine for everyone. Isn't love a wonderful thing?"

With all eyes on her, Margeaux felt the blush spread to her cheeks. Her thoughts drifted to Henri, who was working today. Even the mental picture of him made her heart beat faster.

You have to be truthful with him.

That could mean many things, she justified. It could mean she should be truthful about her feelings for him. It didn't mean she should tell him about the baby.

"Shame on me. I have not even introduced myself. I'm Maya." She took Margeaux's hand. "You are Margeaux Broussard, are you not?"

Margeaux nodded. *Oh, boy, had Maya seen Malone's* Daily Mail *piece?*

"I am terribly sorry for your loss. The entire world grieves with you. I am honored that you have come to my shop in your time of need. I will do everything in my power to help you feel better."

Oh. How nice.

If Maya had read his article, that certainly wasn't the reaction Margeaux would have expected.

The others introduced themselves to Maya almost reverently. Rumor had it that Maya's mother had fancied herself a matchmaker. Maybe Maya had that gift, too—as well as psychic ability.

"What may I get for you?"

Warmth seemed to radiate out of Maya's every pore. Margeaux felt every bit as drawn to her as she did the chocolate Maya made.

"We'd like some chocolate," Caroline said.

"Well, you've come to the right place." Maya gestured grandly to everything and nothing in general. "Did you have something in mind, or would you like for me to make some suggestions?"

The women murmured, each of them gazing around.

"Perhaps some samples, *oui?*" Maya offered.

The women flocked around the wrap stand, and Maya looked at each of them. "All right, let's see…one at a time." First, she looked at Margeaux. "You're the easy one since you're already in love and he loves you, too. So, let's start with you."

The girls squealed.

"I knew it from watching you," said Pepper.

"I called it the first day when I saw his picture in the magazine," said Caroline.

"He was in a magazine?" asked Maya. "Is that true? Is he famous?"

"Does it matter?" asked Margeaux, a little uncomfortable by all the attention. Henri had kissed her, he'd been her rock during the funeral, but nothing had been mentioned about the future beyond his comment about them having left a lot undone when they parted. She refused to read too much into that.

Maya smiled. "You've been through a lot, haven't you?"

It didn't take a genius to figure out that. Her

father had been a well-known public figure and a reporter from the past had reared his ugly head asking about issues that hit too close to home.

But there was no way he could know the truth, despite what he chose to print. She had to stand strong.

And there was no way she was going to jump to romantic conclusions about Henri and have her heart broken again.

"My chocolates have medicinal properties," Maya offered. "The right piece of chocolate can help a person solve their problems and fall in love. This is the one that's right for you."

She held out a piece of heart-shaped dark chocolate. Margeaux accepted it graciously. Even if it didn't have the medicinal properties Maya claimed, it was still darn good chocolate. Good for the soul.

"This one can help the heart find its way. It's especially helpful when you know what you want, but are afraid to go after it. Go ahead, take a bite."

With all the others looking on, Margeaux bit into the candy. It was the same chocolate with

cinnamon, spices and rose petals that she'd eaten right before Henri had kissed her.

It was challenging for Henri to take time off. Even during the slowest of times he found it hard to get away. He'd been called a workaholic more than a few times in his life with just cause.

This may have been the first time he'd actually made it work so he could leave. But then again, it was the first time he'd had a good reason: Margeaux.

During the time they'd been apart, he'd thrown his heart into his work, keeping an array of women, each more beautiful than the next, lined up for his pleasure. No one had the potential to become serious. Happily single, Henri had kept his little black book in constant rotation. He'd become a master at juggling and somehow managed to keep each and every woman in his life content and coming back for more, yet safely at arm's length.

Sydney had been the closest he'd come to settling, and he hadn't even been able to go through with it with her. She was gone now, headed for Dallas. And though he wished her

well, he'd never been more certain that they'd
been all wrong for each other. He'd said it more
than once but still maintained that she was a
fabulous woman and deserved someone who
would love her the way she deserved to be
loved.

It also struck him funny that Margeaux had
showed up at exactly the right moment—of
course, it had been for her father and not for
him. But for a moment he wondered if his
hesitancy with Sydney had been because he'd
somehow sensed Margeaux's return, because
deep down he'd always known Margeaux had
always been the one for him. He'd never loved
anyone else.

Never had and never would.

Now, as he slammed the trunk on his loaded
car, he got behind the wheel and drove away
from his own home and toward Colbert's to
pick up Margeaux to make the trek to Avignon
that Colbert had mandated.

As he turned up the long, winding drive,
he wanted nothing more than to go away with
her, to get away from the hustle and demands
of work. It had been wonderful meeting Margeaux's friends. It was wonderful the way

they'd stood by her, coming over here and staying longer than they'd planned after her father had passed.

But he was equally glad that they'd said their goodbyes yesterday, that they'd gone back to Texas so that he and Margeaux could have the time they needed to reconcile the past with who they were now.

He had a feeling that even though they'd grown, they were one and the same as they'd always been.

The girls were gone.

They'd left early that morning. After Margeaux had driven them to the airport, she'd come home to an empty house and that's when the magnitude of exactly how alone in the world she was set in.

She'd wasted a good hour wandering from room to room. Though she'd thought she'd reacquainted herself with the house when the girls were there, she hadn't realized just how much of a stranger her childhood home was. It had seemed full of life when her friends' laughter had colored the silence, but without them, the place seemed cold and unfamiliar.

Like a person she used to know, but couldn't remember why she'd once been so comfortable around her.

Adjusting to being alone would simply take time. She knew that, though it didn't make it any easier. So, after she'd packed, she'd gone into the garden to take pictures.

No matter where she was, she felt the most at home behind the lens of her camera. When she'd discovered photography, she'd found a new window to the world. It was always the best approach to getting comfortable with new situations, and rediscovering old ones for that matter.

Even so, she was glad when she heard Henri's car tires crunch the gravel in the driveway outside.

Margeaux left the garden, stashing her camera away as she walked back into the house. Her bags were packed and waiting by the front doors. Before he even had a chance to knock, she was wheeling her suitcase out onto the porch.

"Ready to go?" Henri kissed her on both cheeks. Somehow she found the more formal greeting disappointing compared to the way

he'd kissed her senseless the other night. It was the first time they'd been alone since then, and Henri had been warm toward her, but not with the same passion he'd shown that night. Had it simply been the wine talking? Two old friends seeking comfort in the familiarity of the way things used to be?

Her thoughts drifted to what Maya had said about already having found her true love, and the thought made her stomach turn inside out. But the memory of Maya's suggestion that she be truthful with him flat out made her stomach hurt.

"I'm ready to get out of here, if that's what you mean," she said.

A lot had happened since that kiss. Her father's funeral, the tabloid article, and, of course, A.J., Pepper and Caroline had been there. Not exactly the circumstances to reconnect. But now they were alone and heading out of town. Together. If anything would test the waters, surely this would be it.

The thought made her equal parts nervous and giddy.

"Here, let me help you with that." He picked

up the bag. "While I'm putting this in the trunk, you might want to take a look at this."

He handed her a large envelope.

"Pascal dropped it off this morning. I imagine it's instructions from your father for this leg of the journey."

She opened it and glanced inside, only to see a series of smaller, sealed envelopes. Each one was labeled with instructions as to when they should be opened. Margeaux's hands only trembled a tiny bit as she drew out the envelope labled "Begin."

Chapter Six

They took the auto ferry across the channel that flowed between St. Michel and France. It was a relaxing ninety-minute ride during which they enjoyed a glass of wine and shared a fruit-and-cheese plate in the boat's café.

"I have news," he said.

"You do?" Margeaux absently picked up a piece of apple and bit into it. Her gaze was trained on Henri.

He nodded. "Sydney turned in her letter of resignation. Her last day will be the day before we get back from Avignon."

Margeaux's eyes widened and the thought that the news would make her so happy made Henri smile along with her.

"Where is she going?"

"To Texas, of all places. I think she's going to get in touch with your friends."

Margeaux shrugged. "Well, at least she'll know someone there."

"I'm sure she'll become one of the girls in no time."

Margeaux toyed with the bitten apple slice, looking as if she wanted to say something.

"What?" he asked.

She shook her head. "Nothing."

Then it was almost as if the words bubbled up and out of her on their own. "I'm surprised she went. I really think she had feelings for you."

Henri shrugged. "I've made it perfectly clear where I stand on that issue. She's a wonderful woman who deserves someone to return her feelings. I did not."

"Why not?"

Because I love you. They were both adults. He should just be able to tell her how he felt.

Say those words he could never say all those years ago.

The boat rocked gently as the pregnant question swayed between them unanswered.

The problem was Margeaux was fragile right now. With her father dying and this fact-finding mission thrust upon her, she had a lot to process right now. The last thing she needed was for him to put more pressure on her.

He would tell her in good time. In the meantime, he would show her.

"How do you explain love?" he asked. "Why is it that two people have chemistry and others don't? If I knew the answers to those questions..."

For a fleeting moment, he thought he saw disappointment register in her eyes. But then she turned and looked out the window, squinting at the vast ocean and he couldn't be sure.

"Did you know she will be working for Pepper's father?" Margeaux asked. Actually, he did. And that was fine.

"I guess it will be a win-win situation for everyone."

The boat docked in Nice, France. From

there, it was a two-and-a-half hour drive to the outskirts of Avignon.

She'd been rather quiet on the journey. So, he'd opted to give her space, rather than trying to get her to open up or hold her hand like he had at the funeral or kiss her like he had that night after the dinner.

Even though he longed to do all those things.

Just give her room. Everything will sort itself out in due time.

It was after four o'clock when they finally reached Avignon's rampart walls. The sun was falling in the western sky, and the city was beginning to take on a late-day golden hue as evening bathed the ancient buildings and cobblestone streets in light and shadow. It was perfect light for taking photos and Avignon would definitely be a photogenic city. But she didn't have the heart to ask Henri to stop the car now so that she could disappear behind the camera. Photography was such a solitary endeavor, and right now, she wanted to be with him.

The golden light would return tomorrow.

This moment with Henri would never come again.

Inside the city's walls, they passed shops, homes and several bed-and-breakfasts. It was considerably colder and windier here than it was in St. Michel and bundled-up pedestrians and the occasional bicyclist hurried past with purpose.

Since they were staying for two weeks, Henri had rented a two-bedroom house. It would be much more comfortable and private than a hotel or rented room. Colbert had left money for room, board and incidentals. He'd asked Henri to make the arrangements since he would be more familiar with Avignon than Margeaux would after being away.

Henri turned off the busier avenue onto a quiet road, stopping the car on a narrow cobblestone street lined with mature trees and stone buildings. The house was set off from the street by hedges and a wrought-iron gate.

As he and Margeaux got out of the car, pulled on their coats and walked toward the house, they saw a man in a black coat open the front door of the house and approach them from the other side of the gate.

As Henri waited for him, he glanced at Margeaux and it struck him that for the next two weeks they would be living together. Granted they would have separate bedrooms, but it would be just the two of them in this house. It seemed so natural and it dawned on him that neither of them had questioned it.

In many ways it was like a new beginning.

The rental representative made quick order of giving them the cursory tour, collecting the deposit, giving them their keys and getting on his way. He left a business card with his name and number in case they needed anything.

As far as Henri was concerned, he had everything he needed right here.

The place smelled vaguely of lavender and mothballs, with hints of Margeaux's cinnamon chewing gum. It was clean though cluttered with knickknacks and kitsch—lace doilies, porcelain figurines and paintings that looked as if they might have been done by a local artist. The paintings shared wall space with floral painted plates, rough-hewn needlepoint pieces and framed photographs.

The decorating job was not to Henri's taste,

but to him it was more beautiful than any other place on earth, because Margeaux was there.

They left their bags in the entryway and decided to go out and look for a place to eat. They hadn't eaten since the snack on the boat several hours ago, and they both agreed they were hungry.

They chose a place around the corner from their house, right on the main road. Lace curtains adorned the café's glass door. Henri started to pull open the door but a wild gust of wind caught it and whipped it open, making the string of bells on the glass sing and dance a frantic jig.

"Whoa!" Henri called, laughing. "That's some wind."

When he finally got a hold of it, he held open the door for Margeaux. She stepped inside and was immediately greeted by the delicious aroma of something savory. Her stomach growled in appreciation.

It was warm and cozy inside the café, and a pretty middle-aged woman in a black shirt-waist dress appeared from a back room and greeted them with a cheery, "Bonjour! The

mistral opened the door for you. Please don't let him in."

She laughed.

"Bonjour," they called in return.

"Sorry about that," Henri added. "It got away from me."

"It's no problem," she said. "Happens all the time. Sit anywhere you'd like. I will bring menus to you."

They chose the table by the window and took off their coats because it was so warm in there. By the time they were settled, the woman had returned with menus, a breadbasket and a carafe of water. She placed the items in front of them with a practiced efficiency.

Her warm smile was painted deep red and her eyes were the color of well-brewed coffee, a beautiful contrast to her ivory complexion. She had an ageless look.

"Today's special is *boeuf bourguignon*," she said. "I'll give you time to look at the menu, and I'll be right back to take your order."

When she returned, Henri ordered the steak and fried potatoes and Margeaux the special. Since it was so cold outside, she needed something hearty to warm her from the inside out.

The justification had her thinking about being warmed from the outside in by Henri. It would be nice to feel his arms around her.

Henri plucked a small baguette out of the basket.

"*Mmm,* it's warm," he said. "You have to try this."

She picked up a piece. "I wonder if she baked it herself?"

"Probably."

"I've always wanted to learn how to bake bread." Margeaux tore the crusty roll in half, slathered butter on the hot surface and watched it melt into the tender white crevices. "It just seems so homey."

She swallowed the bite, but rather than devouring the rest of the baguette, she set it down on her bread plate and stared out the window.

Home. Though she'd done an adequate job of supporting herself over the years, she'd never really made her places feel like home. After her mother died, then especially after her father shipped her off to boarding school, every place seemed so temporary. She'd moved around a lot, looking, searching, but never connecting.

The closest she'd come to feeling at home was not in a house, but when she was with Henri.

His arm was resting on the table and on impulse, she reached out and put her hand over his. The gesture didn't seem to faze him. In fact, he lifted his hand and laced his fingers through hers. His palm was warm and his hand felt strong and safe around hers. The action seemed so natural, it was as if they'd been doing it for the past sixteen years.

Had her father really been gone a week? It seemed like another lifetime. As she held Henri's hand, she gazed out the café window and pondered the situation that had kept them apart for too many years.

The cold day was coming to a close. A couple walked by arm in arm with a cloth grocery bag brimming over with what she imagined were the ingredients for their dinner. Two young boys bundled in coats and scarves rolled by on skateboards. A horn honked somewhere in the distance, across the way, an old, stooped woman stepped out from the shop across the street to sweep the stone walk in front of her establishment.

This place was home to these people.

Sadness, weighty and dark, loomed over her. Even though her apartment was back in Austin and her father's house, which was soon to be her house, was back in St. Michel, neither of them felt like home.

She glanced down at her hand in Henri's and thought, *this is what I miss; this is home.*

Pleasantly full and a bit drowsy, they made their way back to the house hand-in-hand. Henri felt as nervous as a teenager on a first date—unsure of where to look or what to do, other than to keep holding on.

Funny, he'd always been the one to take the lead with women. This new role of stepping back and following her lead was…different, but it felt right.

"I can't believe how much colder it is here than in St. Michel," she said. "I'm freezing."

She slanted into him as they walked, and he slipped his arm around her, pulling her in close. They walked home that way, under the light of a huge harvest moon.

When they finally got back to the house, they carried their bags to separate rooms and

exhausted, they agreed to get a good night's sleep so that they would be rested and ready for whatever tomorrow's visit to the orphanage might throw at them.

Their rooms were right across the hall from each other. As they said good-night, Margeaux lingered in the doorway, looking like an angel in her white nightgown.

"Would you sleep in here with me?" she asked. "Just hold me?"

Margeaux must've slept the sleep of the dead, because after she and Henri lay down on the bed, she closed her eyes for what she meant to be just a minute, and the next thing she knew bright sunshine was streaming in through the lace curtains on the windows.

She sat up in the four-poster bed and blinked at the light. Sometime during the night, Henri must have pulled the quilt over her, but he was gone now.

She felt a little silly having asked him to sleep with her, but not *sleep with her*. He was a good sport. But she hoped she hadn't tested his good nature too much.

He'd been a perfect gentleman. The thought

made her wish she could have a re-do of last night, because this morning she wished she would've awakened to his face on the pillow next to her. She could imagine making love to him right here, right now in this big four-poster bed.

"Henri?" she called, but her invitation was met by silence that was broken only by the distant sound of a ticking clock somewhere in the house.

She pushed away the covers and glanced around the room. It was small and bright. The walls were painted simple white and adorned with paintings similar to the ones in the living room. But the bedroom walls were remarkably clutter-free. The room was furnished with an economy of furniture: a mirrored dressing table with a delicate stool, an overstuffed chair in the corner and a bench with a cushion at the foot of the bed.

Her gaze fell on the packet of sealed envelopes. She scooted to the edge of the bed and picked them up. There were ten white letter-size envelopes bound together with a rubber band. The instructions on them said to open

them at the end of the week spent at St. Mary's Orphanage.

She slipped one from the bundle and held it up to the light. The stationery was fine ivory linen that didn't give away any clues.

She was going to play the game her father's way. So, she pushed it back into the collection and returned the stack to its larger holder, setting it aside for now.

She set her feet on the cold floor and shivered as she walked to the window and pushed back the curtains. It was another sunny day. The window looked out on the front of the house. The yard was artfully landscaped with plants that seemed to be holding up under the cool weather. There was a birdfeeder hanging from a tree and a birdbath, but it didn't have any water in it. The hedge was tall enough to screen out the street—even though yesterday it seemed to be a sleepy road.

That's when she saw Henri come through the gate with what she hoped were two cups of coffee and a bag of something for their breakfast.

Shivering, she stepped away from the win-

dow before he could see her, and pulled clothes out of her suitcase and dressed in haste.

She wanted Henri, but she needed coffee. Not only to warm her up, but to help her think straight. It was time to get her head together so she could get to work.

She checked the time on her cell phone: seven-thirty. Just enough time to eat, shower and get over to the orphanage to meet Père Steven for their nine-o'clock appointment. No time for anything else that might tempt her to spend the morning in bed.

She made her way into the kitchen where Henri was putting the bread and pastries out on a plate.

"Well, good morning." He sounded cheerful. "Did you rest well?"

There didn't seem to be any traces of resentment or weirdness in his voice. Relief flooded over her.

"I did, thank you. How about you?"

"Like a baby." He smiled. "Coffee?"

"You're my hero." She accepted the cup he offered, and their hands brushed. The skin on skin contact made it suddenly very hard to breathe. Yet she didn't know why. They'd held

hands last night and, well, they'd been much more intimate than that all those years ago.

Suddenly it was very clear to her that she didn't want to be just his friend. She didn't want to walk the same line between friends and lovers and have him not want to venture far past friendship.

She was forming the words to say *About last night*...when he looked at his watch and said, "We'll need to leave here in about forty-five minutes to make it to St. Mary's by nine."

He was right.

No sense in bringing it up now. Especially not before an appointment with the priest. Somehow it seemed improper.

St. Mary's of the Universe was a gorgeous, rambling shambles of a sixteenth-century castle situated on the outskirts of Avignon on acres of rolling land. From a distance it looked fairy-tale perfect. Or, at least that's how it looked through the viewfinder of Margeaux's camera.

In the direct sunshine when the wind wasn't blowing, it was warm, and she was tempted to stay outside and hide behind the lens of her

camera. This was such a photogenic old ruin. She could easily give up an afternoon photographing it.

"I don't mean to rush you," Henri said, apologetically, "but it's nine o'clock right now."

The two of them approached the large wooden doors, each adorned with an open-mouthed lion's head.

Margeaux snapped one last shot of the brass guardians of the door, before she stepped over the threshold into the world where her father had sent her. The castlelike atmosphere made it look like a scene from a *Harry Potter* book. Teenagers hurried past, presumably on their way to class since most of them carried notebooks and backpacks.

These poor kids were here because they were unwanted; they didn't have anyone else in the world to claim them. Her heart clenched, and she felt a sudden kinship with them, even though they didn't notice her. They just hurried on by.

She wanted to take photographs, but now wasn't the time. She drew in a deep breath, and smelled nutmeg, eucalyptus, decay and something she recognized, but couldn't quite

put her finger on…maybe it was the smell of despair.

They followed the directional signs to the administrative offices, where they were met by a woman who seemed too harried and frazzled to have time to help them.

"We have a nine-o'clock appointment with Père Steven," said Margeaux.

The woman glanced up at them, then at her watch.

"Please, have a seat." She pointed to a row of chairs along the wall where a boy waited. He balanced his elbows on his knees and hung his head as if he shouldered the weight of the world. His body language screamed that he was in trouble and he knew it.

As they approached the chairs, he scowled up at them, not really connecting with either of them. He looked about fifteen, dark curly hair and penetrating chocolate eyes. Something about the kid made Margeaux's breath hitch. Then she realized, if she squinted her eyes, he resembled Henri as a boy. The same tall, lanky build, similar coloring.

Her heart ached. This was what their son might've looked like.

When the boy's gaze met Margeaux's directly, he looked away and resumed the too-cool-for-school posture he'd had when they walked in.

Margeaux couldn't stop staring at the kid. She knew she should be more discreet, but she couldn't help it. Especially since the boy wasn't paying any attention. He seemed to be caught up in his own problems, which seemed to be significant once a man wearing a priest's collar opened the door to an office and glanced out. He had a kind face and thinning hair. He was significantly older than Margeaux and Henri but younger than her father.

The stern secretary gestured toward Margeaux and Henri with an obviously irritated flick of her wrist.

"Père Steven, there is your nine-o'clock appointment. But I must insist that you deal with this situation first." She pointed at the boy with her nose.

"Matieu?" The priest's voice was gentle compared to the woman's. "Is there a problem?"

When the boy didn't answer, Père Steven looked at Margeaux and Henri and said in an equally pleasant tone, "Good morning, I'm

terribly sorry to keep you waiting, but will you please pardon me for another moment?"

Margeaux smiled, and Henri said, "That's not a problem. Take all the time you need."

While Henri was speaking, Margeaux angled the camera which was in her lap ever so slightly so that it pointed toward the boy, whose face was visible in profile. She pressed the shutter release button.

The boy's head whipped toward her, shooting a dubious glare first at her and then at the camera. He must have heard the camera's click when she snapped the photo.

Her heart thudded. If he asked she'd simply tell him it was an accident and she'd delete the image if he was really bothered by it. But before he could say or do anything, Père Steven said. "Matieu, please step into my office."

As the boy stood, he kept his suspicious gaze on Margeaux's camera. She wondered what he'd do if she snapped another—because this was the angle at which he most resembled Henri—but the boy seemed to already be in enough trouble. She didn't want to add to his problems by antagonizing him.

Ten minutes later the boy and Père Steven

emerged from the office. Matieu lifted his gaze to give Margeaux and her camera one last glare before exiting.

"Did you deal with him sufficiently?" the woman demanded.

"Mrs. Cole, that will do. We have guests." Père Steven's tone was commanding enough to get his point across, but gentle enough to not be severe. The woman checked her posture then pursed her lips as she busied herself at her desk.

Margeaux and Henri got to their feet. Père Steven smiled at them. "You must be Margeaux Broussard. I've been expecting you."

Chapter Seven

As Père Steven gave them a tour of St. Mary's, Henri was struck by his compassion and enthusiasm for the children. He truly was their champion.

"I am responsible for about two hundred children," he said with obvious pride. "We get by the best we can."

As they returned to the office, it floored Henri that so many children were alone—well, not really alone, because they had Père Steven—but without at least one of their natural parents. It struck him that technically, he and

Margeaux were orphans—adult orphans who had lost both of their parents. Henri's father had passed away about seven years ago; before that, Henri's mother had been tragically killed by a criminal that Henri's father had helped bring to justice. While it was sad, at least his parents had wanted him. It was hard to look at these kids and think no one wanted them.

Even though Margeaux and her father had been estranged, it was becoming clear that Colbert regretted the years they'd been apart and was making it clear that the family bond was important.

Since they'd arrived at the orphanage, Henri had been analyzing everything, trying to figure out why Colbert had sent Margeaux here. Maybe the *family bond* issue was what he hoped Margeaux would take away from her time at St. Mary's.

They still had a week to try and discover Colbert's purpose. Who knew…it might even be spelled out in the letters Margeaux was supposed to read tonight.

In the meantime, he intended to keep his eyes and ears open for clues.

* * *

Later that afternoon when they returned to the house after spending the morning at St. Mary's, Margeaux's cell phone rang, and Pepper's name popped up on the LCD screen. She was glad to hear her friend's voice and was eager for a talk. Henri must have understood this, because he volunteered to go to the market to fetch supplies for their dinner, leaving Margeaux alone to talk to Pepper.

"Hello, darling. I'm calling to wish you an early happy Thanksgiving."

Thanksgiving? Oh, my gosh!

Wait… It was Monday…Monday of Thanksgiving week! How could she have forgotten? She'd been so busy. Sure, it wasn't a traditional French holiday, but it was one of Margeaux's favorites—it was her father's favorite, too—and now that she remembered, she fully intended for Henri and herself to enjoy a traditional meal. Although, without A.J. to prepare the feast, this year might be interesting.

Margeaux took the phone into her bedroom and stretched out on the bed, settling in for a good catch-up session with her chatty friend.

"You'll never guess who's spending the holiday with us," Pepper said.

"Who?"

"Guess! Oh, you'll never guess. So, I'll tell you. Your good friend Sydney."

"*My* good friend? I wouldn't say that. I don't think she likes me very much."

"Oh, well, there was the tiny matter of Henri being in love with you. But you really should give her a chance. She kind of grows on you. And you know I don't make friends easily. She's fitting in wonderfully at Texron. But enough about her. What are your plans for the holiday?"

"Technically, it's not really a holiday over here, but we do intend to feast on turkey."

Suddenly, she was overcome with a fabulous idea. Even if she didn't fully grasp the reason her father had sent her to St. Mary's, she was touched by the place, nonetheless. The troubled look in Matieu's eyes haunted her. She glanced at the stack of still unopened letters resting on the dressing table. Her camera sat right next to them. She got up and retrieved it, flipping back through the shots she'd snapped that day until she came to the one of the boy in profile.

"You do know we're in Avignon now, right?" she asked Pepper.

Pepper made noises that indicated she understood.

"My father has sent me here to see St. Mary's orphanage. I still haven't quite figured out why. But you just gave me a brilliant idea."

Pepper laughed. "Yes, I do tend to have that effect on people. Or so I've been told."

"I have some money saved up, and I want to use it provide a Thanksgiving dinner for the kids in the orphanage."

"Oh, like a dinner party."

"A very large dinner party," Margeaux qualified.

"How large, hon?"

"Two hundred-ish, counting the kids and the staff."

Pepper gasped. "Are you out of your everloving mind?"

"Yes, actually, I'm beginning to believe I am. Do you think A.J. can send me some recipes?"

When she and Pepper hung up, Henri still wasn't back. Margeaux got up and walked over to the letters. She picked them up and held

them, but her instincts told her to put them down. She wasn't sure if she was dreading the actual reading part or what she might learn after she began the arduous task. Her gut told her it was the latter. Reading had always been a chore, but it wasn't as if she was illiterate. She could read and read well when she concentrated.

Since it was so quiet in the house, she decided that now would be as good a time as any to find out what her father hadn't been able to tell her face-to-face.

The first couple of letters were dated around the time that she'd run away from the French boarding school—around the time that she'd miscarried. Her soul gave a little twist at the memory.

When she broke the seal on the first letter, she saw that it was hand-written and she caught a whiff of the unmistakable scent of orange blossoms. Or at least she thought she did.

But orange blossoms in November? She didn't realize orange trees grew in Avignon. Even if they did, this was hardly the season for them.

She held the envelope up to her nose, but the paper smelled slightly of her father's pipe tobacco. There wasn't a trace of the floral fragrance that had been her mother's favorite scent.

She wondered if perhaps she'd just imagined it and settled back on the bed to read by the natural light filtering in through the windows.

The tone of the first couple of her father's letters was slightly reprimanding, explaining how badly she'd not only hurt him, but how she was also hurting her own future.

But gradually as the dates on the letters progressed to the time that she graduated from the American boarding school—the time when she and her father lost contact—the letters became more conversational.

He wrote: "These are the things I would say to you if I could talk to you…."

I loved your mother as I've never loved anyone else. She was my first love, my last love, my only love.

She understood you because the two of you were cut from the same cloth.

When we lost her, you reminded me so
much of her and all I'd lost, it was more
than I could bear.

In the midst of reading, Margeaux heard
Henri come in and vaguely recalled him stick-
ing his head in the bedroom door, only to qui-
etly leave her to her reading.

That was a good thing because what she
learned gave her pause. She needed time to
digest it.

"So, let me get this straight," Henri said
as he and Margeaux worked side by side in
the kitchen, chopping vegetables for a salad
niçoise. "Your father lived at St. Mary's as a
boy? It was his home?"

Margeaux nodded. "I'll show you the
letter."

"Your father was an orphan and you never
knew this?"

"My father barely spoke to me, Henri. All
he ever said was that his parents were dead. He
didn't like to talk about them, so I never pressed
him. I suppose to him they'd never been alive
since he'd never known them. However, in the

last letter he said his mother was a teenager when she got pregnant, and she was forced to give him up for adoption at St. Mary's."

Colbert Broussard was a very proud man. Henri had never heard anything about the man's past, but given the circumstances Margeaux had outlined, he wasn't surprised Broussard had kept everything quiet.

He was such a well-respected "family man." While his wife was alive, his heritage had never come up. Crown Council members were appointed, not elected. While it was very important to the St. Michel government that all Crown Council members be above reproach, Broussard was the epitome of respectable.

But the more Henri thought about it, being put up for adoption was no reason that a person should be disqualified from making a life for himself—especially a life that involved public service. A man had no control over the circumstances of his birth.

Even so, Colbert had guarded his past with a jealous vengeance. Probably driven by the same instinct that had him protecting his future by sending his daughter away.

When Margeaux went through her "phase,"

as certain members of the Council referred to it, Colbert was already ensconced in government. He was a respected public figure and a widower to boot. Sympathy was on his side. Margeaux was the hellion. When Colbert sent her away, he'd done what was expected of him. He'd cleaned up the mess, silenced the hullabaloo.

Despite how he understood the drive that made Colbert do what he had to do, Henri also understood how this revelation might come as a shock to Margeaux.

"How do you feel about all this?" he asked.

She stopped chopping and pressed her hip into the counter, looking thoughtful.

"It's really strange. Discovering my perfect father, who sent me away for being less than perfect, felt like he had something to hide."

She looked at him for a moment, unsaid words hanging pregnant in the air. "Do you remember the night that started it all?"

Did he remember? That day had set the gold standard for all lovemaking to come. It was a hot August. The kind that seems like it will drag on into forever. They'd been lying in the

grass by the lake behind the orchard. The two of them had no place to be and no one to report to.

"It was your idea to skinny dip," he said, the memory of it making him hot. He set down the knife and turned to face her.

"It most definitely was." She was looking at him in a way that had him gripping the edge of the counter to keep from reaching for her. "My idea. But I seem to remember you being a willing participant."

"Are you kidding me? It must have been one hundred and ten degrees outside that day."

She took a step toward him.

Henri wrapped his arms around Margeaux and dusted her lips with kisses that trailed down her throat.

"Oh, you have no idea the things I remember." His voice was a horse rasp.

Her sultry smile teased him, invited him, and unleashed a need that had him searching for what they'd shared all those years ago. He longed to tell her exactly how he'd imagined kissing her mouth…reacquainting himself with her body…burying himself deep inside

her, exactly the way he'd done it that day at the lake.

But before the words could find their way past his lips, she took his hand and led him to the bed where they'd slept last night, where he'd held her, breathed her in, loved her with his mind and heart as she slept.

His hands locked on her waist, taking possession of her body.

She tucked herself into his chest. He buried his face in her hair, breathed in the scent of her—that delicious smell of flowers, amber and the green of the vegetables they'd been prepping. A scent that was so familiar, yet new, that it hit him in a certain place that rendered him weak in the knees.

He breathed her in and melted with the heat of her body.

"Make love to me, Henri."

Smoothing a lock of hair off her forehead, he kissed the skin he uncovered, then searched her eyes. She answered him with a kiss, a silent *Yes, I want this.*

Relishing the warmth of her, and the way she was clinging to him, he cradled her face in his palms and kissed her softly, gently, until

her fingers found his. She laced their fingers together. Their hands lingered a moment, gripping, flexing, hesitating, as he silently gave her one last chance to object, to escape, to run away from what was about to happen.

But she wanted it to happen. She'd been waiting for this to happen again since the last time she'd kissed him. Her lips parted on a sigh and gave him full permission to take possession of every inch of her.

A rush of red-hot need spiraled through her. He must have read it in her face because he let go of her hands and his arms encircled her. In a fevered rush, he claimed her mouth, her thoughts, her sanity. Her fingers slipped into his hair and pulled him close, closer until they were kissing with a need so furious it was all consuming.

She clung to him, relishing the closeness. There was no mistaking his need or his desire, as his hands swept down the outer edge of her body to claim her bottom.

Then somehow, in a heated whirl of passion they tugged away their clothes—her blouse, her skirt, his shirt, his jeans—until they'd gotten

rid of every barrier between them so that they stood naked and wanting.

Together.

He held her so close that she could hear his heartbeat. She felt safe and at home for the first time in years. With every fiber of her being she concentrated on the moment, shoving away the dark curtain of the past that threatened to close between them. The voice that chattered about how there was too much water under the bridge. About the things she hadn't told him.

But all she wanted was *this*.

Right now.

Not the past.

Not the future.

The present.

Right now.

His lips found hers again, and she shut out everything else but the need that was driving both of them to the brink of insanity.

He kissed her neck, and her fingers swept over his broad shoulders and muscled arms, before reacquainting her touch with the curve of his derriere. She pulled him even closer so that the hardness of him pressed into her, urging her legs apart, searching, proving his need.

He eased her down onto the bed. It was crazy how much she wanted him. Utter madness.

Above her, he claimed her mouth again, capturing her tongue, teasing her, pulling away to smile down at her. His lips were swollen and red, and she desperately wanted to taste them again.

A warm, calloused palm splayed over one of her breasts. His fingers moved from one nipple to the other then trailed down her belly where they lingered and played, tracing small circles that made her stomach muscles tighten and spasm in agonizing pleasure. Then his hand dipped farther still, teasing its way down her body, edging toward a hidden place that begged for his touch.

His fingers slid inside her, stroking, coaxing one moan after another until one shock after another vibrated thorough her and she couldn't be without him any longer

She ached for him, needed more.

So much more.

As if he heard her unspoken plea, he reached over and grabbed his pants, pulled a condom from his wallet and rolled it on. He covered

her body with his, and she marveled at how perfectly they'd always fit together.

His first thrust stole her breath, drove her deliriously mad. As his own moan escaped his lips, his gaze was locked on hers, and he slid his hands beneath her, helping her match his moves in and out of her body.

Each strong, bold, shameless thrust took greedily, but gave back so much more, until they both exploded together in an ecstasy the likes of which she'd never known.

As they lay there, sweaty and spent, Henri collapsed protectively on top of her. For the first time since she could remember, she knew what it felt like to be loved.

Chapter Eight

Margeaux could finally breathe, and her tension had floated away like a piece of paper on a gust of wind. Never before had she had so much to be thankful for. Despite losing her father, she felt as if she knew him better than she ever had in her life.

And then there was Henri. Things had never been better. They still connected on a level like no other. She was in love. She'd never stopped loving him. Now she could safely admit that to herself.

The next morning at St. Mary's, she and

Henri sat in Père Steven's office and presented the idea for the traditional Thanksgiving dinner.

"It's a lovely thought," he smiled sadly. "However, we cannot afford to stray from our current menu. We've already spent the week's budget on food."

"Will the food keep?" Henri asked.

Père Steven weighed the question. "Much of it is canned or frozen. So, yes, the majority of it will."

"We are prepared to buy the turkeys and the other ingredients needed to give the children a treat," Margeaux said. "We're prepared to roll up our sleeves and help, too. In honor of my father, a boy who lived here and went on to build a good life for himself. Think of it as a way for me to celebrate his life."

Père Steven said he would have to check with the kitchen staff to make sure the cafeteria manager was on board with the idea.

Soon, the school was abuzz with word of the special meal that the visitors were providing.

That day, Henri had some conference calls to attend to, so after their meeting with Père Steven, he went back to the house to get some

work done. Margeaux stayed to help in the library. She'd also talked to Père Steven about taking photographs around the school and the common areas of the orphanage later that day when the light was right. But first, she would assist the librarian as she'd promised.

She was reshelving a stack of books when she saw Matieu sitting at a table by himself drawing in a notebook. He looked up from his work and caught her watching him.

He got up and walked over to her.

"Why did you take a picture of me yesterday in Père Steven's office?" he asked her in French.

Margeaux shrugged as she formed her answer in French. "Because I'm a photographer. That's what I do. Would you like to see it? I have my camera right here."

She pulled out her camera, which she'd stashed on the bottom shelf of the cart. Matieu scowled at the camera, then at her, his expression wary as if he didn't know if he should trust her. For some strange reason, she understood his hesitancy.

She found the shot and held out the camera to him. "Here," she said. "Look."

He wrinkled his nose when he saw it but stared at it for a while.

"What are you going to do with it?"

Margeaux took a book from the cart, looked at the title, then the Dewey decimal number, because it was painful to look at this boy and not think about the child she and Henri might have had. "Nothing. Would you like to have a copy of it?"

Her offer seemed to catch the boy off guard. "Well, I don't have any money to buy it off you, if that's what you mean."

He was a tall boy, all feet and big hands with long, awkward limbs he hadn't yet grown into. Just like Henri had been at that age.

"Oh, no, that's not what I meant at all. I'm happy to give you a print. Have you ever had a photograph of yourself?"

She stole a glance at him in time to see him shake his head.

"Well, Père Steven has given me permission to take photographs around the school. If you'd like, maybe I can shoot some more one afternoon after school this week?"

He leaned on the shelf, propping his arm up and resting his chin on his fist, as he sized

her up. He seemed to be getting a little more comfortable with her now.

"Do you work here now or something?"

She considered the question and how to best answer it. She didn't need to bog him down with the hows and whys of what she was doing there. "I'm only here for a week helping out."

"So then if you're going to take my picture it has to be, like, tomorrow or something, right?"

She nodded. "Yes. Would you like that?"

"Yeah, that sounds cool."

Tuesday night, Henri and Margeaux went on a scavenger hunt for turkeys, buying up every bird they could find.

A.J. had said to allow for about one pound per person.

Finding fifteen twenty-pound birds might have been a challenge had the school's cook not been on board with the plan and directed them to a poultry farm about ten miles outside of town.

So by Wednesday, they had all the components they needed for their traditional turkey dinner. Armed with A.J.'s recipes, some of

which had been adapted by the school cook to utilize ingredients on hand and to expand the recipes to feed an army of hungry kids, Henri and Margeaux helped with the prep work until they'd helped the cook and her staff get everything under control.

The next day's menu would include turkey and stuffing, mashed potatoes and gravy, green beans and pumpkin pie.

After they were finished Margeaux managed to spend some time photographing Matieu, as she'd promised.

Of course Henri had no idea why Margeaux was so smitten with the kid, but she came home that evening full of stories and talking about how sad it must be for these teenage kids who never would have a chance to be adopted by a loving family.

"If circumstances were different," she said as they relaxed on the couch, enjoying a bottle of wine he'd picked up in the market. "I'd consider adopting him."

She had so much love to give and it was touching, but sitting there, just the two of them, he couldn't imagine anyone intruding on their lives.

He put his arm around her and she snuggled into him.

Henri knew this wasn't real life; he understood it was what he considered a "snow globe" moment: a snapshot in time, a perfect moment in the perfect setting, insulated from the rest of the world.

Their "snow globe" time was speeding by. The day after tomorrow would be their last day at St. Mary's before they moved on to the Saint James convent so that Margeaux could learn the next piece of untold family history or whatever it was that Colbert had in store for her.

He nuzzled her hair. It smelled clean, like fresh flowers.

Learning about her father's past had been meaty stuff, and, thank God, it seemed to be helping Margeaux get through losing him. Henri hoped whatever came next would be as beneficial. That it would be something Margeaux could take with her—even if it was only in her heart.

They hadn't talked about what would happen after they returned from Avignon. Whether she would go back to Texas or stay in St. Michel.

But as he kissed her neck, working his way around to her mouth, all he wanted to do was make love to her.

The Thanksgiving feast was a success, and with great regret, Margeaux bid farewell to Père Steven, Matieu and the rest of the people she'd met at St. Mary's.

She'd been so busy at the orphanage helping and taking photographs, she hadn't had time to see much of Avignon. Therefore, when Henri suggested they spend one last day to play sight-seers, she jumped at the chance.

She hadn't been to the city since she was a kid. One summer, on one of the rare vacations her family had taken, they'd come to Avignon.

It was one of those memories that seemed as if it had been ripped out of a photo album: her mother and she at a café table; a mental image of herself on the steps of the Pope's Palace; a dreamscape of her mother sniffing a bouquet of lavender.

Her father must have been the photographer, because there were no pictures of him, and Margeaux couldn't remember any accounts

of him being there—except for his ghostlike presence. He was there, he had to have been because they wouldn't have gone on vacation without him—which was why they rarely went—but unlike the vivid recollections of her mother, she really had no accounting of her father in Avignon.

She had snapshots of memories, but she wasn't sure she actually remembered, or if she'd conjured the recollections after seeing photographs.

That's why on this day that she and Henri had set aside to play tourists, armed with her camera, she wanted to see if any of the sights jogged memories. They went on foot and spent the entire day exploring every inch of the city: they saw the Pope's Palace, which, as the guidebook promised, dwarfed the cathedral; they shopped on Rue des Teinturiers, the famed artisan street, and in the open-air markets where Henri had been purchasing the fruits and vegetables they'd been enjoying; she had Henri snap a photo of her sniffing dried lavender—a recreation of the one of her mother, and she purchased some pure lavender oil, because it was good for relaxation.

She photographed the opera house, and they visited the various museums. Finally, after a full day, they hauled their tired bodies down to the river and had a picnic by the Avignon Bridge. The bridge was actually named Pont Saint-Bénézet Sur, but was immortalized in the famous nursery rhyme as Le Pont d'Avignon.

Unfortunately, by the time they got down there, the afternoon had turned cold and gray. Sullen clouds in the moody afternoon sky seemed to be as fed up with the wind's battering as the rest of the locals. Instead of settling themselves on a patch of grass near the Avignon Bridge, Henri and Margeaux headed upstream a bit.

"Where are we going?" she asked.

"It's a surprise," Henri said.

Just around the bend, the tree-lined street opened into an expansive field where several colorful hot-air balloons brightened up the landscape.

"How about a balloon ride?" he asked. "We saw the city at ground-level. It'll be fun seeing it from the sky looking down."

It was one of the most romantic suggestions ever.

"How did you arrange this?" she asked.

"I saw a flier at one of the markets and I thought it would make a nice surprise…so *voilà*."

They took their picnic in the balloon with them, opting to toast each other as the balloon pilot took them up, up, up over the city until the ramparts and the village looked like a tiny toy town.

The balloon pilot must have been good at romantic flights, because he rendered himself all but invisible, turning his attention toward the horizon opposite Margeaux and Henri as they sailed over the top of Avignon.

At the altitude at which they were traveling, it was significantly colder than it was on the ground. Henri put his arms around Margeaux.

"Body heat," he said.

Despite all that had happened between them, their sharing a house and bed in Avignon, the rekindling of their physical relationship, they hadn't talked about the future. Up there, from that vantage point—or maybe it was the sheer romanticism of sipping champagne as Henri held her close so far above the

earth—Margeaux was suddenly at a loss for words.

She could get used to this.

And that worried her.

They hadn't talked about the future but the burning question looming in the back of her mind was, *What's next for us? Where do we go from here?*

The question was building but was blown away by the wind before she could form the delicate foreign sentence.

It was interesting how, when she kept busy with projects and deadlines, she could block out the little voices that meandered through the back of her mind. But when she let down her guard, stopped the idle chatter, the voices tended to seep into the crevices of her heart.

Voices that warned her not to let Henri break through the brambles that had grown around her broken heart, holding together the pieces. Because if she did, one of two things would happen: she might make the mistake of believing that her broken heart had been put back together and was whole again; or her heart might simply fall apart and she might not be able to feel again.

What is next for us?

She didn't know.

Because the wind was kicking up again, and the cold was chilling her to the bone.

Henri leaned closer and wrapped his arms around her tighter, trying to shield her from the biting cold with his big body. He was so warm and smelled vaguely of cedar and leather, and something clean and green.

She could so easily get lost here in his arms. She could forget herself. And she did, for a while, as he ducked his head and found the sensitive spot at the base of her neck, before he finally claimed her mouth. His lips were hot and sensuous, and they warmed her up from the inside out, despite the way the wind was blowing and demanding to know: *What's next for us?*

And the question—or maybe the possible answers—made Margeaux shiver.

"What's wrong?" Henri asked.

How did she tell him? How did she explain that she had no idea what she was doing? That she wanted him, that she wanted *this,* but she had no idea what *this* was—if *this* was real, because it had certainly never lasted before.

In fact, every time in the past *this* had ended so badly.

He gazed down at her with such intensity, his brown eyes squinting against the wind. He looked so open. Yet, for all his patience, how could she expect a man like him to want to make a life with a broken woman like her?

He pressed her fingers to his lips. Kissed her fingertips, slowly, one by one. And the biting wind swirled around them, as if tying them together.

"It's okay," he said, as if reading her mind. "They say the Provençal wind does strange things to people. It can turn them inside out, seduce them, make them do things they'd never dream of doing."

"As if that's ever been a problem for me," she retorted.

His eyes gleamed with mischief as he pulled her into him, kissing her. In that moment with the wind in their hair, she could pick out the amber and umber in his deep brown eyes. Right then, more than ever, he looked like the boy she used to know.

He kissed her deeply. It was a scorching kiss, and the heat of it reached all the way through

the brambles and thistles that had grown around her broken heart. A searing kiss that made her feel.

Yes, she thought, maybe the wind *could* seduce people and incite feral thoughts and untamed dreams about the awakening of love. But she knew better. Most of the time it whispered promises it never intended to keep.

It whispered secrets: secrets kept, secrets that should be told. But the past was like the sudden spray of dried-leaf confetti that had danced away on the breeze down by the river; the future was the strong arms holding her, keeping her warm as they floated above the earth and all its problems.

As the balloon made its approach, preparing to land, she watched as the wind whipped the water across the Rhone, brewing whitecaps that resembled waves on the Mediterranean. This was only a small, imaginary ocean and she could see the shore on the other side. She wondered as she sat there shivering, if that might be a good omen. It was funny how when she stopped focusing on herself—her own problems, the little voices that had always chattered in the back of her mind, insisting she wasn't

good enough because she was stupid, a screw-up—those voices quieted when she focused outward rather than inward.

They'd also been nearly nonexistent since she'd been with Henri.

But as the balloon basket landed with a thud, the fickle wind changed directions and blew her hair into her eyes.

Suddenly the voices of doubt were back. What seemed so clear moments ago now made her feel restless and anxious.

Another packet of letters arrived via courier on Sunday, but as with the bundle of letters that had preceded the visit to St. Mary's, the letter that accompanied this bunch came with a note from Colbert, instructing Margeaux to visit the convent before reading the letters.

The following day, they found themselves at Saint James Convent, located about ten miles west of the orphanage. Their appointment was with Sister Jeanne, and she was waiting for them when they arrived.

Henri was surprised to discover that the woman was younger than he'd expected. In

fact, she was probably not much older than he and Margeaux.

Interesting.

She had a pretty face, and a calm, quiet manner. He wondered why she'd chosen this life. He wasn't judging, just curious at how someone could be so sure of what they wanted. Or so sure that they *didn't* want a life's mate—not an earthly one, anyway.

Henri understood the part about not being compelled to settle down with a mate. He'd gone his entire adult life running from just such a commitment. But now that Margeaux was back in his life, he was also beginning to feel a tug in the other direction, that sense of free-falling through time and space and into love.

In many ways, it was the opposite of what he'd felt for Sydney—or maybe it was more apt to say what he *hadn't* felt for her. The emotions that Margeaux evoked were at once compelling and overwhelming.

While he enjoyed the comfort and ease they naturally slipped into, he craved her like the body thirsted for orange juice when it needed vitamin C or hungered for bread when it needed nourishment.

She nourished his soul.

As Sister Jeanne shepherded them around the convent, Henri found his mind wandering to thoughts of how much he wanted to hold Margeaux's hand or taste her lips, both of which he refrained from doing in this holy house in front of women who had pledged the vow of chastity.

When their gazes snagged as they trailed along with Sister Jeanne, he could tell that Margeaux was thinking the same thing.

When they paused in the chapel, Margeaux sniffed the air. There it was again. That phantom scent she thought she'd smelled as they entered the convent. But as they'd gotten engrossed in conversation, the aroma had faded and she'd forgotten about it.

Until now, when she was sensing it again.

"Do you smell orange blossoms?" she whispered to Henri.

He shook his head.

It must have been a note in Sister Jeanne's cologne. Did nuns indulge in cologne?

Perhaps it was her soap.

Or maybe flowers adorning the chapel. But

when she glanced around, she didn't see any bouquets decorating the place.

When they exited the chapel, a black sedan that was parked across the street caught her eye. In many ways, it was just an ordinary, unremarkable car, but the dent in the driver's-side door set it apart. Now she was sure it was the same car she'd seen parked across the street from St. Mary's and then again yesterday near the market as they'd walked around Avignon.

Today, a man was slumped down in the front seat. He had a cap pulled down over his forehead and sunglasses, so it was impossible to get a good look at him. What she got instead was an uneasy feeling. She'd had to circumvent enough reporters in her younger, wilder days, it was almost as if she'd built up a sixth sense for them.

But why here? Why now? Visiting a convent and the tourist magnet of Avignon was hardly newsworthy.

Still, when another nun came to tell Sister Jeanne there was an important phone call she needed to tend to, she left Margeaux and Henri alone to enjoy the courtyard as they waited.

"Henri, over the past couple of days, have you noticed that car over there before?"

She turned to point at it, but by that time it was gone. It had evaporated in the same manner as the phantom scent of orange blossoms, leaving her wondering if both had been figments of her imagination.

Until Henri said, "Are you talking about the beat-up black four door that was over there a moment ago?"

He'd seen it, too.

She pointed at the empty space. "Yes that's the one."

"I noticed that same car yesterday, downtown. Strange that he's here again today."

A few moments later, Sister Jeanne came back.

"I'm terribly sorry you had to wait," she said. "Let's go into the living room and have some tea. I have a lot to tell you about your mother and the time she spent here. And I'm sure you'll have a lot of questions."

Chapter Nine

Her mother had intended to become a nun?

The revelation had floored Margeaux. She was surprised but not flabbergasted by her father's secrets. However, even though Margeaux was only sixteen years old when her mother died—and not necessarily privy to adult aspects of her mother's life—she thought she knew her mother pretty well.

How could it be that her mother also had an entire secret past she'd kept from her daughter all those years? One Margeaux knew nothing about until now? Especially given that,

Margeaux soon learned, *she* was at the center of the secret.

Over tea, Sister Jeanne had outlined that Margeaux's mother, Bernadette Loraine, had been a novice at Saint James and had intended to take the vow until she was lured away by love.

It sort of sounded like the *Sound of Music,* except the man who tempted her was not a widowed captain with seven singing children. No, there had only been one child when her seventeen-year-old mother left, and that child would be named Margeaux Simone Broussard.

Her mother had been pregnant when she ran away with Margeaux's father to start a new life. Considering her parents' meager upbringing and her father's rise to political success, the two had done well for themselves.

Margeaux didn't understand why her father would be so ashamed of his past. The last packet of letters hadn't addressed it. She could only assume that his obsession with perfect appearances made him ashamed of the fact that he'd lured a seventeen-year-old girl away from a convent, and he'd gotten her pregnant in the process. Those in high-ranking public

office had committed far worse infractions and kept their careers intact, but on the return trip to St. Michel, Margeaux had reviewed the letters and reflected on her visits to the convent and orphanage. She'd come to one conclusion about her father.

He was a perfectionist.

He wanted nothing less than the perfect life for his wife and daughter. Perhaps by wiping the slate clean of past infractions, he thought he could accomplish just that.

In the letters, he never went into the hows and whys, he'd simply narrated a story about the past and left her to draw her own conclusions. He also told her that the information was hers to do with as she pleased. Since both he and her mother were no longer living, she could use her best judgment as to who would know about their family history.

It was a conclusion to the past that seemed to edge right up to where Margeaux's installment of Broussard history began. Her father never knew she was pregnant. However, given her father's illegitimate birth, her parents' conceiving a child out of wedlock and then Margeaux's

own teen pregnancy—history seemed to keep repeating itself.

Would the cycle of unwed pregnancy end if she confessed her miscarriage to Henri?

Or would it simply open old wounds neither of them could do anything about?

She walked into her father's study with the last letter in the stack she'd opened during the convent visit, settled herself on the couch and reread it:

Dear Margeaux,

Now you have a clearer understanding of who your father and mother really are. I won't try to explain away the reasons we did what we did. We were young and in love and sometimes that combination can have life-altering consequences.

However, don't think for one moment that I would have changed anything about our past—even if I wasn't keen on publicizing it to the world. I understand at times it may have seemed as if I didn't want you. That was as far away from the truth as one could possibly stray.

True, you and I were very different people. I wanted you to read books, but you
were too busy exploring the world around
you. But please know that I respect our
differences and have made peace with the
fact that you have always been your own
person.

I sent you away because I saw how in-
fatuated you and Henri were. By the time
the tabloid reporter publicized your rela-
tions with him, I realized the best thing I
could do for you was to remove you from
the situation. As I said, sometimes love
can blind a person's best judgment. There
is no way to tell young adults who believe
that they are in love that sometimes people
change and grow in different directions.
I feared you would decide to throw your
entire life away on a childhood crush, so
I had to separate you and Henri so that
you could experience life apart. If you
were truly meant to be, you would end
up together.

What I did not bargain on was the estrangement. If I made any mistakes that

I wish I could go back and change, that is the one. But it's easy to see the right decision when you're staring down the barrel of the past.

We will never retrieve those lost years, and for that I am deeply sorry. If it is any consolation to you, please know that I always loved you—even if I neglected to show you. My love for you never wavered and will remain eternal.

Please accept my gift of the past. Do with the history what you will and always remain true to the beautiful person you are.

With eternal love,
Your Father

For a long time, she sat and stared at her father's fine handwriting. Her dyslexia made the letters and words appear to jump around on the page, but she'd read this letter so often that she was more or less reading from memory.

Even though her father wasn't physically here to experience this with her, really, it felt like the first time she had ever connected with

him. The first time that each of them understood where the other was coming from. She wondered how he would have reacted if he had known about her battle with dyslexia. But in the end, she decided it was better to enjoy the knowledge that her father accepted that they were simply different people. Even so, he had still respected her for who she was, even though she was not like him.

That in itself relieved a mountain of guilt and sadness.

Henri and Margeaux had been home two days when he received a phone call from Pascal Moreau, Colbert Broussard's attorney.

Pascal invited Henri to join him for lunch in a private room in the University Club to discuss what Pascal deemed "urgent business."

They made small talk over a lunch of lamb chops and herbed green beans—a little heavier than Henri was used to for the noon meal, since he usually grabbed lunch on the fly. After being away for two weeks and having mountains of catch-up work to do, he really should have had a quick sandwich at his desk today. But according to Pascal, the issue could not wait.

Once the server had cleared the lunch dishes and brought the coffee, Pascal pulled out an official-looking file and opened it on the table.

"This is an addendum to Colbert Broussard's last will and testaments," he said. "If you'll remember, in the initial reading of the will, Colbert said that if you completed the task he asked of you there would be something in it for you."

Task? Was the man serious? Spending two weeks in Avignon was no *task*. It was heaven.

"Look," he said, pushing back from the table. "I don't want any part of Colbert's estate. It should all go to his daughter."

Pascal looked perplexed. "I'm afraid this particular...err...gift is nontransferable."

"Then give it to charity," Henri insisted. "I will not accept anything from him for simply accompanying his daughter on the fact-finding mission he sent her on, even one as worthwhile as the trip turned out to be. Thank you for lunch. I need to get back to work."

Henri stood. The trip was *worthwhile* to both Margeaux and him. It helped him realize how he'd never stopped loving her, and suddenly,

sitting there alone with her father's attorney, he realized that if he didn't want to lose her all over again, he'd better make sure she knew darn good and well how he felt.

As soon as he got out of there, he'd call her and ask to see her that night.

"Please sit down, Mr. Lejardin," Pascal said. "I'm afraid this is something completely different than what you're thinking."

Henri lowered himself into the chair. "What is it?"

"There's a letter." Pascal held up an envelope. It was the same ivory linen stationery that Colbert had used for the letters he had written to Margeaux.

While they were in Avignon, she had offered to let him read them, but he'd declined. She'd shared a little bit about their contents, about her father living at St. Mary's and her mother being a novice at Saint James. And, of course, Sister Jeanne had provided some of the information.

However, instinct had warned him that what the letters contained that hadn't been spoken aloud was intensely personal and when Mar-

geaux wanted him to know the rest, she would share it.

For now, Henri was giving her time to come to terms with everything that had been unveiled.

Pascal pushed the envelope across the table to him. Henri picked it up tentatively, held the crisp weightiness of the fine stationery in his hand, looked at the florid penmanship that spelled out his name—Henri Lejardin—across the front.

Tentatively he broke the seal that held the flap in place.

Dear Henri,

Years ago, you were like a son to me. I regret the time that we have not been on good terms, but for reasons I do not wish to divulge, it was necessary. You must trust me.

However, I have watched you grow into a capable, reliable businessman who has earned my respect and it is my honor to give you my endorsement for my vacant seat on the Crown Council. Proper noti-

fications have been sent to those involved in the nominating process.

I wish you only the best for your future and believe that you will serve your country well.

Deepest Regards,

Colbert Broussard

Henri was astounded and elated to have secured Colbert's nod. That evening, he read the letter aloud to Margeaux. She was the only person who would understand the magnitude of how much this meant to him.

"Your father...I just can't believe he could go from barely speaking to me to *this*. This is the Crown Council. I certainly never expected it this soon, and without his official endorsement, who knows when I would have had another shot at it."

"You'll make a wonderful Councilman," she said.

He shook his head. "I need to slow down. I don't have it in the bag. This is simply the beginning. Now they have to do their due diligence and make sure—"

She put a finger to his lip. "*Shhhh...*tonight

we celebrate. Come with me down to the wine cellar and help me pick out something to celebrate your imminent victory."

She grabbed his hand and led him to the door just inside the kitchen. Everything seemed electric—a sultry note in her voice, the earthy smell of the air as she opened the wine cellar door, the feel of her hand in his. They descended the dim, narrow passageway that led to the dank, dark room below. Henri glimpsed the way their bare hands were laced together— skin on skin—the contrast of his big, rough hand on her smooth flesh. There was something agonizingly intimate and familiar about it.

His mind raced back to a night long ago. Colbert was entertaining…some head of state from a country Henri couldn't recall at the moment. Margeaux had led him down to the cellar because they were going to sneak a bottle of her father's wine out and drink it down by the lake.

But once they were down there and they'd flipped the switch to turn on the light, the bulb blew with a quick pop and hiss.

Margeaux had giggled and the sound of her

laugh had echoed in the small, earthen cavern, only to be snuffed out as Henri pressed his lips over hers and then claimed her body, backing her up against a far wall, making love to her as muted sounds of the party played like a radio off in the distance.

The memory made Henri suck in a deep breath to quell the rush of need that flooded his body. His fingertips twitched against Margeaux's skin as the wave of desire overtook him. In the dark cellar, they were teenagers again—young and wild and free.

"Don't turn on the light," he said. His voice sounded husky and hungry. And he was ravenous for her.

With the hand that was holding hers, he drew her into him without a word. His lips instinctively found their way to hers. He knew those lips—even in the dark. He smelled the scent of her that intoxicated him, and another surge of need coursed through him.

She did things to him—wonderful, stupefying, mind-blowing things that turned him inside out with need. Margeaux Broussard had had that affect on him since the first day they both were old enough to understand that a man

and a woman could be oh, so much more than friends.

He loved these lips. He's kissed them in his dreams over the years she was away—now that he had her here again, the thought of losing her again was almost too much to bear.

She tasted of the cinnamon gum she favored and another, honeyed sweetness that was hers alone. It was a familiar taste, a timeless taste, because her lips belonged to him.

She was the yearning he'd felt, the scent he'd desired, the taste he'd craved in his soul of souls.

Groaning with need, his hands roamed her body with a greed he'd never experienced—not even years ago when they were so familiar, so comfortable with each other.

She was hot and greedy, too. Her hands traveled over his body, tracing his face, his shoulders, his arms, as if memorizing the shape of him.

They kissed in the shadows, shutting out Crown Councils and orphanages and convents—putting on hold the past and the future to live in the very heady present.

The now.

He wanted her. Now.

Their ragged breaths were the only sound in this dark, sheltered world. Dim light filtering down from the top of the stairs was the only illumination. He kissed her with his eyes open, seeing only her in his mind's eye.

He tugged her sweater over her head, driven by the need to feel the intimacy of her breasts in his palms.

She unbuttoned his shirt and he shrugged out of it, pulling her close as he let it fall to the floor. He wrapped his arms around her tighter, unable to get close enough to her, relishing the warmth of skin on skin. He kissed her lips, her neck, her collarbone, her breasts, sinking to his knees as he worked his way down to the waistband of her jeans.

He unzipped them and pushed her jeans and her panties to the floor in one swift move. She stepped out of them and uttered a soft groan as he kissed her stomach and moved his hands around to the back of her, burying his face in the damp, warm, ready center of her. His penis nudged at the imprisonment of his pants, responding to the primal aphrodisiac of her.

He urged her legs apart and tasted her until

she arched back, crying out in pleasure as tremors made her whole body quake at his touch.

She urged him up and helped him out of his pants, which he caught before they hit the ground. Since she'd returned, he was sure to keep at least one condom on him always. He felt his way to it in the dark.

By the time he'd readied himself, his eyesight had adjusted ever so slightly to the darkness. He led her to that place in the corner where they'd made love so many years ago. Though they'd made love often while they were in Avignon, tonight it felt brand-new all over again. He entered her with such a sense of desire, he couldn't remember wanting her this much or...ever feeling so much love.

"I love you," he said.

"Henri," she whispered, his name, but it was half-strangled on a moan, as he filled her slowly, savoring how right she felt, how the two of them fit together in perfect oneness.

They began to move together. Finding their pace, they reached a new height of ecstasy. After they climaxed, and they stood sweaty and spent, she finally found her voice.

"I love you, too."

* * *

The flurry that surrounded Henri's political approval was nearly as overwhelming. Once word leaked out that he was the heir apparent—no one seemed to know exactly where that leak started—Henri became the toast of the town.

If all went according to plan, he would be the youngest Crown Council member in the history of St. Michel.

He'd wanted this, yet never dreamed that he would get it so soon. With Margeaux here to share it with him, everything he wanted seemed to be lining up perfectly.

Until he found himself at the center of a tabloid scandal that could ruin everything good in his life.

Chapter Ten

Rory Malone had struck again.

The headline that darkened the front page of the *Daily Mail* read: Heiress and Future Crown Council Member Reunite With Son They Gave Away as Teen Parents.

Underneath the tabloid headline, on the left side of the page, was a grainy photo of Margeaux and Henri with Matieu at St. Mary's Orphanage. On the right side was a copy of a page from a hospital chart bearing her name and the medical complaint: pregnancy-related complications.

The gist of the story was that Margeaux and Henri had a baby, but the child was put up for adoption and the boy still lived at St. Mary's. He had been a hindrance to this politically hungry family's plan. They'd left him there to free themselves to further their own causes.

Malone took the opportunity to trot out a retrospective of various other scandalous photos of Margeaux over the ages, including the one of Henri and her skinny dipping—the one that started the tear in her relationship with her father.

Now it was coming back full-circle to tear apart her relationship with Henri, as well.

Henri had found out about the article first. When he did, he'd called Margeaux to warn her about the "bogus story." She'd managed to make noises she hoped were convincing enough to lead him to believe that she, too, thought the story was a bunch of rubbish.

"Of course, it's caused some concern," he said, sounding only mildly bothered by it. "It will delay the process. More than anything, St. Michel wants its Council member to be above personal reproach. They'll investigate and when they discover it's all a bold-faced lie,

proceedings will continue and our attorneys will deal with the paper."

"I am going to make sure they suffer big for this one."

The only problem was, only half of the story was a bold-faced lie—as Henri had put it. The other half—the part about the pregnancy complication—was one hundred percent factual.

Margeaux had no idea how the slimeball Malone had gotten his hands on her medical records, or if exposing it to the world was even legal, that was a matter for the lawyers.

But if he was able to publish the medical information, the photograph of the page from her chart would contain everything the Council needed to discover that she had indeed been pregnant when she left here sixteen years ago.

Not only would the embarrassment be a possible blemish on Henri's record, but it would reflect badly on her father.

Because he was gone and not able to defend himself, Margeaux felt all the more protective of him. He'd worked hard his entire life to protect his name and to keep his private life private. Who knew what Rory Malone would

dig up and expose next? Evidently humiliating Margeaux seemed to have become his life's work.

Margeaux knew she needed to figure out what she would say to Henri. How she would explain to him why she'd chosen to keep the pregnancy a secret when she'd been sent away and why she hadn't trusted him enough to tell him about the miscarriage.

Henri's day seemed to be going from great to horrible. This morning, he'd awoken in the arms of the woman he loved. Now he was sitting across from her listening to her tell him that half the tabloid story was true?

She had indeed been pregnant when she left St. Michel for the boarding school in France all those years ago.

He felt something akin to fury rising in his throat, but he swallowed it. At least he had the foresight to know that if he indulged in losing his temper he would regret it later.

Much in the same way Margeaux was saying she regretted not telling him she had been carrying his child when she'd left and shut him out of her life.

"Is Matieu our son?" he asked cautiously, bracing himself for the answer.

Margeaux stared at her hands for a moment. "No, he's not. I had a miscarriage after I ran away from the school in France."

Henri didn't know whether to get up and hold her or get up and leave.

She'd left with his child. Who knows if he would have ever found out if unfortunate circumstances hadn't brought her back?

"Did your father know?"

She shook her head. "Nobody knew, except for the people at the hospital."

"And obviously the reporter. Why did he wait until now to share the news?"

"How am I supposed to know that, Henri? All I know is I tried to tell you I was pregnant the night before I left. Do you remember that? Do you remember what you told me before I could?"

She paused and in the silence, memories of that night flooded back to him.

When she'd started talking what he thought was nonsense about them running away together, he'd broken up with her. He'd told her since she was going away, it was time that they

needed to be free. He was coming at it from the angle that they needed to spread their wings and grow up a little. After all, they'd always been each other's everything. They didn't know anything else.

Another thing Margeaux didn't know was that her father had gotten to him before she had. It was almost as if Colbert had been able to read his daughter like a book. He'd warned Henri that she would ask him to help her run away. He'd threatened Henri, saying that if he got in the way of his plans for Margeaux, not only would Henri suffer serious consequences, but Colbert would see to it that his entire family was ruined.

"Now the whole world knows about the antics of your skinny dipping with my daughter," he'd said. "This has the potential to ruin her and me and if that happens, not only will I make sure you never see my daughter again, I will make sure you and your family suffer ten times worse than we do."

Henri Lejardin had never been a coward. He had, however, been a smart kid. Colbert Broussard was a powerful man. He was not someone to be trifled with.

Henri had let Margeaux go.

"I didn't tell you because you broke up with me and then I miscarried and what good would it have done for you to know?"

He started to protest, to tell her everything he should've said to her that night, but she silenced him with a wave of her hand.

"I've always felt guilty about the miscarriage. I felt like it was my fault since I was so bent on running away, that I put too much stress on my body and I didn't get proper prenatal care. But most of all, Henri, telling you wouldn't have changed anything since the damage was already done."

They agreed they needed to think about things. To process everything. After Henri left, for a long time Margeaux sat alone in the quiet kitchen of the house that had quit feeling like her home after her mother died.

She'd lost her family and a piece of herself when her mother died. And when she'd gotten pregnant, she'd felt as if through the miracle of having her own child—as unconventional and unexpected as the pregnancy was—she could finally be whole again.

She and Henri would be a family and there would be so much love. Everything would be all right again.

But it hadn't worked out the way she'd planned it.

Her father had sent her away. He hadn't even known she was pregnant, yet he still didn't want her.

He was better off without her and had proved as much by being successful all the years she was out of his life.

But since her recent visits to the orphanage and the convent, all she'd learned about her family had made her feel that they were with her once more. That she was finally home once more. And now, as the sun set and cold, gray darkness crept into the kitchen, it dawned on Margeaux what she needed to do.

Henri spent the better part of the night pacing.

Pacing and thinking.

Though a lowlife tabloid reporter had chosen to twist facts, stretching them out of proportion, there really was no scandal.

Matieu was not his and Margeaux's son.

Yes, there had been an out-of-wedlock teenage pregnancy sixteen years ago, but they hadn't broken any laws. The pregnancy was a private matter that had no bearing on the government of St. Michel.

Last night he had been shocked to learn about the child he and Margeaux had conceived. He'd been angry that she hadn't trusted him enough to share the secret, to allow him to shoulder some of the pain with her, or that she hadn't at least wanted to lean on him through the hard part.

But he had chosen his team when he'd followed Colbert's orders of letting Margeaux go without a fight.

As the sun rose on a new day, one of the first things he decided was that he wouldn't tell Margeaux he'd stayed away because of her father's mandate.

Sure, it might be looked upon as one more secret between them. As him doing something similar to what she had done. But after she'd made such positive strides toward feeling good about her relationship with her father, he decided he would take that secret to his grave—and unlike Colbert, he wouldn't

someday share it posthumously with his and Margeaux's children.

That was the second realization he'd come to: he wanted another chance to have a future, and children, with Margeaux. Even if it meant giving up his chance for a seat on the Crown Council.

Margeaux Broussard was the love of his life, and there was no way he would lose her again. He put on his coat to walk next door to tell her so, but when he opened his door, an ivory linen envelope fell from the doorjamb and landed at his feet.

When he picked it up, he recognized Margeaux's handwriting. He tore it open and read:

My Dearest Henri,

For better or worse, you have always been the man I love. To prove the depth of my feelings, I need to give you room to distance yourself from me.

Even after laying low for so many years, I still can't seem to get away from Europe's tabloid press. In Texas, I did

manage to have the closest thing to a normal life that I've ever had.

You have a brilliant career ahead of you. If you think about everything, my father's career thrived when I left. If I'd come home, I would have destroyed him.

So, I will return to Texas and leave you in peace.

Yours always,

Margeaux

The St. Michel Airport was quiet when the taxi dropped off Margeaux at 6:00 a.m. Even though the ticketing booths didn't open until eight, the place never closed. Sure, it would be mostly uninhabited at that hour, but she would be the first in line to get her ticket—not that there would be long lines, of course.

Ticket lines mean nothing. Truthfully, Margeaux simply didn't want to take the chance of Henri seeing her leave, of her looking into his disappointed eyes and saying goodbye again. Or even worse—if by some miracle he'd found it in his heart to forgive her for not trusting him with the news of the pregnancy and for ruining

his career—she didn't want to give him the opportunity to talk her out of leaving.

Because it would only take one word to convince her: *Stay.*

The airport's main building was located on a slight hill that allowed a perfect view of the water running like a dark, lacy ribbon along the coast of St. Michel. Dawn wouldn't break for at least an hour, and the lights of the early risers were beginning to click on, dotting the coast with a subtle golden shine. If she squinted her eyes at the glowing houses and the stars twinkling in the inky, indigo sky reflecting off the water, the tableau offered an impresson of Van Gogh's "Starry Night Over the Rhone."

Normally, Margeaux would have whipped out her camera to capture such a picturesque scene, to preserve it, possibly even sell it for personal gain. But this moment seemed sacred, too precious to share. It was a memory she wanted to keep for herself, so that anytime she felt as if she were losing herself she could retreat into her mind's eye and remember St. Michel exactly the way it looked right now— sleepy and peaceful, somehow unchanged and

resistant to the ugliness of the tabloids and the misunderstandings of the past.

She sighed and gazed up into the hills that overlooked the city, in the general direction of her father's house. Henri was right next door—where he'd always been…where he was right now. Though after the recent turn of events, he probably wasn't waiting for her anymore.

Now that she'd failed him, he could finally move on.

If only she could do the same. But that seemed unfathomable right now.

Pressing a hand to her aching heart, she turned away from the picture-perfect landscape, committing it to memory before the harsh light of reality marred it even more, robbing her of this keepsake.

She started at the man standing behind her, gasping and flinching at the unexpected surprise.

He was dressed in a khaki uniform, with the St. Michel crest emblazoned on one breast pocket and the word *Sécurité* boldly spelled out on the other.

"Excusez-moi, Mademoiselle," he said. "May I please see your ticket?"

Margeaux's grip tightened on the handle of her suitcase. She mustered a smile she didn't quite feel. "I don't have a ticket yet," she offered. "I was waiting for the counter to open."

The guard, a beefy fellow who looked to be in his late thirties, did not smile. He shook his head and regarded her sternly as if she were a small child caught in the act of doing something naughty.

"In that case, I must see some identification."

They had no right!

Margeaux stewed as she sat in the locked airport security room, held prisoner without reason. Or at least no one seemed to be able to give her a reason.

Since when had waiting to buy a ticket become a crime? The guard had informed her that national security forbade "loitering in the airport common areas."

Huh? What about the legions of passengers who would be waiting for flights once the sun was higher in the sky?

Then he'd escorted her to the small, stark

office with a desk and three plastic-and-metal chairs. The place looked eerily like a detention room.

"I assure you, I mean no harm," she said. "I just arrived a little early. I can leave and come back, if that would make you feel better."

The guard sized her up for what seemed hours, and before she could pull the *do you know who my father is...err...who my father was* card, the realization that her father was gone rendered her speechless. The awareness was akin to being punched in the gut, but before she had a chance to recover, the guard was backing out of the room, saying, "So sorry, Mademoiselle. You must remain here until further notice."

"You can't hold me prisoner," she said, finally finding her voice.

"It's a matter of national security. Wait here. Someone will be with you momentarily."

When *momentarily* had stretched into more than a half hour, she tried the door, only to find it locked.

How could she be a threat to national security? What the heck was going on?

She rattled the handle and pulled hard. To no avail. She was locked in.

Had they forgotten her? Had that horrible Rory Malone made up something else that might make national security believe she was truly a threat?

Ugh… She sank down into a chair. This was all the more proof that Henri was better off without her. In St. Michel—actually, in all of Europe—she couldn't escape scandal. Henri deserved better than that. He *needed* better than that.

At least in Texas, with the support of Pepper, A.J. and Caroline, Margeaux had managed to piece together a normal, if uneventful, life.

Texas was where she needed to be now.

But before she could leave the tabloids and all the hurtful scandal behind, she had to get out of this office.

She pounded on the door for a good ten minutes, knocking and yelling, "You can't keep me here without telling me why you're holding me."

Finally, the door flew open, and Henri was standing on the other side.

Margeaux gasped, both grateful to be freed

and unnerved at seeing the man she loved so desperately—but couldn't have.

Then, she was even more confused when he pulled her into his arms and smothered her mouth in a kiss.

She was stunned at first, but in a heartbeat instinct kicked in and she was kissing him back.

"I am so glad I got here before you left," he murmured between kisses.

Her heart leaped at his words. He wasn't mad at her anymore—

But wait—his lips were still on hers and he dusted her bottom lip with a feather-soft kiss.

She pulled away.

"Did you have security detain me?" she demanded.

He shrugged, a mischievous glint in his brown eyes.

"You had them lock me up in here, Henri? Told them I was a security threat?" She started to turn away, but he pulled her into him with one strong arm around her waist.

"Shhhh…" he pressed his fingers to her lips. "I'm sorry for that. Of course you're not a security risk. Luc told them to use whatever

means they needed to hold you so you wouldn't leave. Margeaux, I couldn't let you slip away again. Not after missing you for half our lives. We have enough lost time to make up for. We can't afford to lose any more."

Before she could sort the right from the wrong, the anger from the relief, the desperate tug of war over getting away from this man whom she loved so much and wanting to be with him...

Henri dropped down on one knee and was holding both of her hands in his.

"Margeaux, I want you with me always. Please say you'll be my wife."

Her heart nearly burst with love. Every fiber of her wanted to say yes, but she couldn't. She loved him too much to do that to him.

"Oh, Henri, there is nothing in the world I want more than to say yes and spend the rest of my life with you. But we both know what that will cost you. You will never be able to have your dream if we're together. Even more important, you'll never be able to have a moment's peace in your life."

He got to both feet, still holding her hands in his, the most earnest look on his handsome

face. The emotion in his eyes threatened to break her heart.

"Your father guarded your family's private life viciously. I promise you with every fiber in my being that I will do the same for our family. No harm will come to you. I promise you."

She shook her head and tried to pull away, but he wouldn't let her go. In fact, it surprised her when he pulled her closer and gazed into her eyes.

"You think this is what you want now, but, Henri, I'm a magnet for scandal and you don't deserve that kind of life."

The way he smiled at her nearly broke her heart. She wanted nothing more than to be with him, to find herself in the dream-come-true of being his wife. For then she would truly be home.

But she loved him enough to let him go.

Then, as if reading her mind—he'd always been so good at that because they were *that* connected—he said, "All you have to do is look me in the eye and say that you don't want me— that you don't want *us*—and I will let you get on that plane. But, Margeaux, you and I both

know the true scandal would be losing each other again. So what's it going to be?"

"*Ooh—*"

He dropped down to his knees again. "Please say you'll be my wife."

He wanted her.

Even after all that they'd been through, he accepted her for who she was, for better and worse. He *still* wanted her. The slow-dawning realization warmed her from the inside out, thawing the doubt, quelling the urge to run. It would take trust and faith in each other, but—

"Yes. Yes! I love you. I have always loved you and I always will. There is nothing that would make me happier than being your wife."

Epilogue

Simple blood tests proved to the council that Matieu was not Henri and Margeaux's natural son. However, after Henri won his seat on the Crown Council, he and Margeaux were married and adopted Matieu and brought him to live with them in St. Michel.

Margeaux sold the photographs she took at St. Mary's Orphanage to an internationally renowned magazine and donated the proceeds to the orphanage.

This inspired her to set up her own phil-

anthropic organization, which she called the Fille Sauvage Charitable Trust.

Two of Margeaux's first Fille Sauvage projects were trusts in the names of Colbert and Bernadette Broussard to honor her parents' memories and to fund the organizations that had shaped them in their formative years.

Margeaux Broussard's philanthropy earned her an international reputation, generating many positive stories in newspapers and magazines.

In exchange for releasing the *Daily Mail* from a libel suit, the tabloid agreed to no longer report on Margeaux, and Rory Malone was fired from the paper.

* * * * *

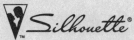

COMING NEXT MONTH

Available November 30, 2010

SPECIAL EDITION

#2083 A THUNDER CANYON CHRISTMAS
RaeAnne Thayne
Montana Mavericks: Thunder Canyon Cowboys

#2084 UNWRAPPING THE PLAYBOY
Marie Ferrarella
Matchmaking Mamas

#2085 THE BACHELOR'S CHRISTMAS BRIDE
Victoria Pade
Northbridge Nuptials

#2086 ONCE UPON A CHRISTMAS EVE
Christine Flynn
The Hunt for Cinderella

#2087 TWINS UNDER HIS TREE
Karen Rose Smith
The Baby Experts

#2088 THE CHRISTMAS PROPOSITION
Cindy Kirk
Rx for Love

REQUEST YOUR FREE BOOKS!

2 FREE NOVELS PLUS 2 FREE GIFTS!

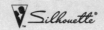

SPECIAL EDITION

Life, Love and Family!

YES! Please send me 2 FREE Silhouette® Special Edition® novels and my 2 FREE gifts (gifts are worth about $10). After receiving them, if I don't wish to receive any more books, I can return the shipping statement marked "cancel." If I don't cancel, I will receive 6 brand-new novels every month and be billed just $4.24 per book in the U.S. or $4.99 per book in Canada. That's a saving of 15% off the cover price! It's quite a bargain! Shipping and handling is just 50¢ per book.* I understand that accepting the 2 free books and gifts places me under no obligation to buy anything. I can always return a shipment and cancel at any time. Even if I never buy another book from Silhouette, the two free books and gifts are mine to keep forever.

235/335 SDN E5RG

Name _____ (PLEASE PRINT) _____

Address _____ Apt. # _____

City _____ State/Prov. _____ Zip/Postal Code _____

Signature (if under 18, a parent or guardian must sign) _____

Mail to the **Silhouette Reader Service:**
IN U.S.A.: P.O. Box 1867, Buffalo, NY 14240-1867
IN CANADA: P.O. Box 609, Fort Erie, Ontario L2A 5X3

Not valid for current subscribers to Silhouette Special Edition books.

Want to try two free books from another line?
Call 1-800-873-8635 or visit www.morefreebooks.com.

* Terms and prices subject to change without notice. Prices do not include applicable taxes. N.Y. residents add applicable sales tax. Canadian residents will be charged applicable provincial taxes and GST. Offer not valid in Quebec. This offer is limited to one order per household. All orders subject to approval. Credit or debit balances in a customer's account(s) may be offset by any other outstanding balance owed by or to the customer. Please allow 4 to 6 weeks for delivery. Offer available while quantities last.

Your Privacy: Silhouette is committed to protecting your privacy. Our Privacy Policy is available online at www.eHarlequin.com or upon request from the Reader Service. From time to time we make our lists of customers available to reputable third parties who may have a product or service of interest to you. If you would prefer we not share your name and address, please check here. ☐

Help us get it right—We strive for accurate, respectful and relevant communications. To clarify or modify your communication preferences, visit us at www.ReaderService.com/consumerschoice.

SSE10R

HARLEQUIN®

A Romance

FOR EVERY MOOD™

Spotlight on

Classic

Quintessential, modern love stories
that are romance at its finest.

See the next page
to enjoy a sneak peek from
the Harlequin® Romance series.